#1 *NEW YORK TIMES* BESTSELLING AUTHOR

JESSICA SORENSEN

Awakening You

a Novel

For information:

jessicasorensen.com

Cover Design by Okay Creations

Photographer: Perrywinkle Photography

Awakening You (Unraveling You, #3)

ISBN: 978-1507680674

Chapter 1

Ayden

"I want you to close your eyes and relax," my therapist instructs in an even, soothing voice I've heard at least a dozen times.

I'm lying in a lounge chair in front of him with my arms overlapped on my stomach, and my heart is slamming against my chest as I prepare to be put under for my amnesia therapy. The soft flow of the ocean drifts from the stereo, and birds chirp just outside the window beside me.

"Relax," he repeats. "Clear your mind."

Clear my mind.

Clear my . . .

Body . . .

And . . .

Mind.

I fall deep into my thoughts, a blanket of darkness wrapping around me.

Around.

Around.

Around.

"Ayden!" my sister cries from the recliner. "Stop spinning me so fast."

I continue to lap circles, pushing the chair she's in. "You asked me to spin you, so I'm spinning you."

"Not this fast, though!" she cries through her laughter, gripping onto the torn armrests. "I'm going to throw up!"

"Oh, fine." I stop moving and hop back, watching the chair continue to twirl until it gradually slows to a stop.

"That was fun." She bounces from the chair, her arms spanning to the side as she staggers toward me. "Whoa, I'm so dizzy." She braces her hand against the sheetrock wall beside her. "Everything looks all blurry."

I laugh, sitting down on the edge of the scuffed up coffee table. "Give it a minute, and it'll stop."

She nods, sinking back into the chair. "So, I heard a rumor about you."

"Oh, yeah?" I ask, vaguely interested as I pick up the

remote and turn on the television. The service has been turned off, though, probably because my mom forgot to pay the bill again, so I turn it off.

"Yeah, I heard you kissed Laura Flemming on the lips." She giggles.

I set the remote down. "So what? It's not that big of a deal."

"That's not what I heard." Her eyes sparkle mischievously. Sadie has always been the kind of sister who likes to tease me about everything. "I heard that she wants to be your girlfriend."

I roll my eyes. "Well, she can tell me that herself, then."

"That's such a boy answer."

"If you haven't noticed, he is a boy." My older brother enters the living room from the hallway. He's wearing plaid pajama bottoms, and his hair is messy, as if he just woke up, even though it's six o'clock at night. "Where's Mom?"

I shrug. "Out."

He shakes his head, aggravated and exhausted from the late hours he's been putting in at his job and school.

"Probably doing drugs."

"She doesn't do drugs," Sadie spits. "Stop saying that she does."

"You're just in denial," my brother replies, winding around the chair and heading for the kitchen attached to the living room.

"I am not."

"Am, too."

"Would you two knock it off," I intervene, being the peacemaker as always. "Just let her be, okay? It's not that big of a deal."

"Yeah, it is." He motions around us at the shithole we've called home for about a year now. "Look around you. If you can't see how bad things are, then you're dumb as fuck."

"I'm not dumb." Tears overflow from Sadie's eyes. "Why do you always have to be such a jerk?"

He sighs. "Look, I'm sorry, okay? I just want you to see how things really are so maybe you can have a chance at a better future."

"I know things are bad," she mutters, "but it doesn't mean I have to be all mopey about it all the time."

I hate when they fight. Life is bad enough already.

"How about we go outside," I suggest to Sadie, "and see what kind of trouble we can get into?"

Sadie beams as she springs from the chair. "Can we go see Miss Tammy's puppies?"

"Sure. Why not?"

She bounces off toward the door while I shoot my brother a look as I head for the front door.

"Don't ruin her happiness yet," I mutter under my breath as I pass by him. "Let her be a kid for a little while longer."

"She's thirteen-years-old." He grabs a bowl from the cupboard then lowers his voice when he realizes Sadie is still lingering near the front door. "She needs to start growing up and realizing just how shitty our lives are. And how shitty our mother—"

"My babies!" The door swings open violently, and my mother bursts into the narrow living room with her arms wide open. Her attention falls on Sadie, and she lazily grins. "Come give Mama a hug."

"Speak of the devil," my brother mumbles under his breath.

Sadie gives her a nervous, one-armed hug. "I missed

you."

She trips in her heels as she staggers into the small living room. "Where have the three of you been?"

"Right here." My tone is clipped. "Waiting for you to show up and pay the damn bills."

She frowns as she slumps against the wall with her head tipped back, her droopy eyes on the stained ceiling above. "I've been busy . . ." Her eyelids lower as if she's about to pass out. "How long was I gone?"

I bite down on my tongue until the rusty taste of blood fills my mouth, hating myself for detesting her so much. "Four days."

"Four days," she murmurs sleepily. Her head starts to angle to the side, and I think she's about to pass out, but she suddenly gets a second wind. Her eyes pop open as she jumps away from the wall. "I need you guys to come with me."

"I have to go to work," my brother snaps while pouring cereal into a bowl.

"Work, shmirk." She waves him off, staggering over her own feet as she jerks open the front door. "Come on. This is important."

I exchange a quizzical look with my brother, and he

shakes his head and slams the box of cereal down onto the counter.

"Fine, what do you want?" he asks, striding to the front door.

"It's outside," she whispers, her gaze darting from left to right.

My brother rolls his eyes, but steps outside, anyway. "I'm getting so tired of this shit."

My mom stumbles down the rickety porch to the gravel driveway, and we all follow her. The sky is clear, the sun gleaming brightly, but there's a chill to the air.

"What do you think she's on this time?" he asks me as we hike down the windy road, past trailer homes, and toward the field surrounding the area we live in.

I shrug. "I really don't care anymore."

Which is the truth. I may hold it together on the outside, but I was done with my mother and her drug and alcohol addiction a long time ago. I have four more years of this shit, and then I'm getting out. The moment I graduate, I'm packing my shit and leaving. And I'm going to take Sadie, too.

My mother leads us on a wild goose chase up through

the field and around the fence line before heading back toward the house.

"I have a bad feeling about this, Ayden," Sadie whispers to me. "In fact, I had one of my feelings this morning that something bad was going to happen today."

"It's going to be okay." I squeeze her hand, trying to comfort her, but I'm pretty fucking worried myself.

By the time we've reached the road again, I figure my mother probably forgotten the purpose of why she brought us out here—if there was even a purpose to begin with—and is going to take us back to the house.

But she makes a right at the smaller home just next door, and the three of us begrudgingly trail after her, exhausted and cranky and ready to go home. Even Sadie has grown quiet.

"Just wait right here," my mom instructs as we reach the bottom of the rotted, wooden steps that lead to a crooked front door. She climbs up the stairs and fixes her dress into place before knocking.

The door swings open, but I can't see who's inside the house. For the most part, the three of us have tried to stay away from our neighbors, considering most of them deal and do drugs.

I hear hushed whispering and sigh, knowing more than likely my mom's buying drugs. My gaze travels around the area, across the road, along the front of the house. I notice a strange, jagged, circular pattern painted on the metal along with a sign that reads: Enter at your own risk. Those who dare step in never get out.

Part of me thinks the warning is a joke, but a small part of me starts to get a little anxious about who lives in this house.

"Okay, are you guys ready for this?" my mother asks, drawing my attention back to her.

The door to the house is wide open, but the person who answered has stepped back so I can only make out their silhouette and what looks like a head of red hair. It seems so dark and smoky inside, as if there are no open windows or ventilation.

"Go on." She has something in her hand and a nervous look on her face as she flicks her wrist and motions at the door. "Get in there."

Sadie moves forward first, and I hear a cackle from inside. The sound triggers something deep inside me, a warning.

Something's wrong.

Don't go in. Don't go in.

I run for her with my hand extended, reaching to grab her and pull her back, but the house starts to fade away—everything does—and bleeds red.

Bleeds red.

Don't go in there.

Blood.

Don't go.

Blood everywhere.

Close your mind. Trust me, you don't want
to see what's about to happen...

My eyes shoot open as I gasp for air, but my lungs are constricting, and I can't get any oxygen.

"Help," I gasp, rolling to my side, clutching at my chest.

Dr. Gardingdale is above me, his eyes wide as he pats my back and tells me to, "Breathe. Just breathe. Air in. Air out. In. Out."

He repeats the mantra until I calm down, and then he moves back and gives me room.

I sit in the chair with my feet planted on the floor and my head in my hands. "I was remembering the day my mother dropped us off at the house," I finally say. "But the memory would only go up until the point where Sadie ran inside, and I went in after her. Then it shut down . . . All I could see was red."

I hate that, no matter what, my mind refuses to let me see what happened in that house. All I know is a female there had bright red hair and disgustingly long nails. They also didn't—don't—like it when people leave their group, even those who didn't enter of their own freewill.

He studies me closely as the music changes from the sound of ocean waves to the lull of a waterfall. "I think that's going to be all for today." He seems distracted as he stands up from his chair and walks over to his desk. "I'm starting to get concerned, though, that we might be putting too much pressure on your mind." He collects a prescription pad and a pen from his drawer. "I'm going to write you a prescription just in case you have another panic attack like that."

"I won't take the pills." My legs are wobbly, and my stomach is woozy as I push up from the chair and work to get my footing.

He leans over the desk, pressing the pen to the paper.

"I'm not saying you have to take them, but you'll have them on hand just in case."

"She was buying drugs the day she dropped us off. She was high and needed her next fix, so she sold her kids out to a fucking bunch of evil people." I stuff my hands into the pockets of my jeans. "So, trust me when I say I won't take the pills."

He sighs but drops the pen and turns to face me. "Well, just know that the option is there and that there's no shame if you decide to take them."

"Okay." I nod then start for the door.

He scoops up his office keys from the desk. "Let me walk you to your car."

Ever since the incident in the parking lot where a chunk of my hair was stolen, he has been walking me to my car. He always locks his office up first, even though he goes back inside afterward.

After he locks up, we exit the building and cross the parking lot toward my car parked out near the back row, even though the entire area is vacant.

"It was more crowded when I came here," I explain, glancing up at the sky now painted with stars.

"You're usually my last client of the day," he replies,

reading a message on his phone.

When we near the car, I fish the keys from my pocket and push the key fob. The headlights flash across the dark parking lot as the doors unlock.

"I'll see you next Tuesday," I say, pulling the driver's side door open.

He nods absentmindedly as he turns back toward the office building. "Take care, Ayden. And, if you need anything at all, call me."

"I will." I lower my head to climb in but pause when I spot a blank piece of paper on the dashboard. I pick it up and flip it over. Invisible fingers wrap around my neck, and suddenly, I can't breathe again.

Those that step in, never get out. We're going to torture you until you break. Just like we did to your sister.

I drop the note to the ground and scramble back, scanning the parking lot. Even though the note wasn't signed, I know who left it. The Soulless Mileas, a group of people who held my siblings and me captive in that house I saw in the memory just minutes ago.

"Wait, something's wrong," I call out to Dr. Gardingdale. "There's a note."

He reels around, nearly dropping his phone. "Where?"

I point to the ground at the piece of paper, my eyes trained on the trees, the buildings, the bushes, every place someone could be hiding. "They must have put it in there while I was inside," I say as he crouches down to examine it without picking it up. "I don't know how, though. The car was locked."

He straightens his legs and stands up then slowly circles the back end of the car. He walks around the front and down the side, inspecting every inch while dialing a number on his phone. He halts near the passenger side and moves closer, lifting his head to look on the roof. "Your sun roof's open." He glances at me from over the car. "Did you leave it open?"

"Maybe . . . I was honestly pretty distracted when I drove here." Distracted by the heavy make out session I had with Lyric right before I drove here. My thoughts were lost in her and the way her lips felt against mine. How soft her skin was against my hands. The soft whimpers she kept making. "I'm sorry."

"You don't need to be sorry. None of what's happening is your fault." He puts the phone up to his ear and starts chatting with the police to report the incident.

It's the second one he's had to report in two months, and I'm starting to wonder exactly how many more incidents are in my future. If the note holds any truth to it, then probably a lot.

I'm never, never going to be free

Until I die,

Or they capture me.

I'm not sure what ending's worse.

Chapter 2

Ayden

Four hours later, I'm in the police station with Lila and Ethan, waiting for Detective Rannali—the person working my brother's murder case and my sister's kidnapping—to come speak with us about what happened tonight.

"I wish this could have just waited until morning." Lila restlessly jiggles her foot up and down as she scans the busy room full of officers. She has flour on her jeans and shirt because she was cooking for a wedding she's catering when she received the call to come here. "It's too late for him to be out on a school night."

"Honey, I think, considering what happened, it's good that they want to tackle this tonight." Ethan places his hand on her knee to settle her. "Be thankful they're not shoving it aside."

"I am." She ceases bouncing her leg. "I'm just really tired of all of this and those damn people. Why can't they just leave us alone?" Regret fills her eyes as she looks over at me. "Sorry, I know I'm making this worse."

"You don't need to apologize." I slump back in the seat. "Besides, I'm the one making this worse. I brought this on everyone."

"Don't you dare say that," she starts to protest, but stops talking when Detective Rannali strolls up.

His white, button-down shirt is wrinkled, his tie is crooked, and his hair is disheveled. "Sorry to make you wait. It's been a long day." He nods his head at his office door. "Come inside. There's some stuff I'd like to talk to you about."

The three of us simultaneously rise to our feet, file into his office, and take a seat in front of his desk. Once everyone gets settled, he opens a folder that contains the note I found tonight.

"So, ever since this all started, we've been wondering why the Soulless Mileas are so fixated on you—leaving notes, stealing your knife, taking your hair—yet they never actually make any threatening moves. We've had some theories, but we weren't positive." He glances from the note to me. "This note is starting to confirm our suspicions."

"And what are you suspicious of?" Lila asks, grasping onto Ethan's hand for support.

She has been doing that a lot lately, revealing just how much stress this ordeal has been putting on her. It makes me feel so damn guilty all the time because it's my fault. I brought these people into their lives. I brought this stress into their lives.

The detective closes the folder and overlaps his hands on top of it. "When I was first put on your sister's case," he speaks directly to me, "I remembered interviewing this woman in the neighborhood who believed the people who took Sadie stalked her first. She reported seeing people breaking into the house. I didn't look into it too much, because the source had ended up being highly unreliable. But, over the last few weeks, I've been noticing a pattern."

"They're doing the same thing to me." My fingers curl around the armrests of the chair, and my fingernails scrape at the wood. "And, eventually, they're going to try and take me."

Lila gasps, covering her mouth with her hand. "That's

not what's going on," she says in denial.

"I never said that," the detective says with caution. "I just said that there are some similarities between your case and your sister's. And the note, well, it's just more proof that you need to start being extremely careful."

"How can I be more careful?" I ask, dumbfounded. "I already spend no time alone. There's an alarm in the house. My therapist walks me to my car."

"We'll do more to keep him safe." Lila places a hand on mine. "It's going to be okay."

"No, it's not." I stand up, ignoring their protests to come back as I exit the office.

I want to walk out the front door of the station and just start running until my legs give out. Run away until I feel safe. But nowhere is safe, and running away is only going to put me in harm's way. So, instead, I wait for Lila and Ethan by the glass entrance doors. They don't show up for another thirty minutes, and by then, Lila looks like she's been crying.

"Is everything all right?" I ask her as she strides up to me.

"Everything's great." She folds her arms around me

and yanks me close, despite my rigidness. "Everything will be okay."

Lies. Lies.

Everyone lies.

Lies to save me.

Lies to break me.

Lies to make me ache.

How many more lies are in my future?

"What do we do now?" I ask Ethan from over Lila's shoulder as she continues to hug me so tightly I can barely breathe.

"The only thing we can do," he replies, wrapping an arm around his wife. "Go home and make a plan that will keep you safe."

I nod in agreement for his benefit. But no matter how many plans they make, I'll never truly be safe.

Those that step in, never get out.

Never, ever, ever.

Chapter 3

Lyric

The most depressing song of all time is playing in surround sound. Definitely not my choice of music, especially when so much dreariness haunts Ayden's life already. Every day, he's plagued by the fact that the same people who kidnapped him and his siblings over four years ago are holding his sister. The same people have also been tormenting him for the last several months by breaking into his house, stealing his hair, and as of three days ago, leaving him creepy notes in his car.

With my sketchpad propped open on my lap, I stare across the room at him, assessing the pain he tries to keep hidden while drawing the shadows of his smoldering dark eyes framed by the longest, darkest eyelashes I've ever seen.

Today, he's dressed in all black and sporting the leather bracelets that match mine—Christmas presents we gave to each other a few months ago. Each stroke of my pencil captures the pain concealed below the surface of his strength.

As I'm shading his eyes, the iPod shifts to the next song, which turns out to be as equally energy draining as the first.

"Who picked out this playlist?" I climb off the sofa and pad over to the stereo that's below the flat screen mounted on the wall.

Ayden peers up from the notebook he's been scribbling in for over the last hour, sweeping wisps of his inky black hair out of his eyes. "I thought you did."

"Yeah, right. These songs are too depressing for me to be listening to at the moment." I frown at the stereo. "My mom must have turned it on before she took out the sugar junkie clan for dessert."

The Gregory's kids are staying over for the night while Ethan and Lila are away at their son, Everson's, football game. At fourteen-years-old, Everson is living his dream already, playing quarterback for the middle school league. While the Gregorys wanted to take the whole clan with them, they thought it'd be best if they stayed behind, considering it's a school night. Lila acted like a nervous wreck when they dropped everyone off and gave my mother an hour-long lecture about keeping Ayden in the house at all times with the alarm on and an adult always around.

After dinner, my mom suggested everyone go get ice cream, but Ayden and I stayed behind with my dad who retired to his office about thirty minutes ago to put together a band line-up for his club.

I tap the skip button, moving to the next song, "My Heroine" by Silverstein. "Much better."

"Much better?" Ayden cocks his brow. "It's as slow as the last one."

I hold up a finger. "Give it a minute." I sway my hips to the slow rhythm of the song while sweeping my hands through my hair. When the tempo quickly picks up, I grin cockily at Ayden. "See. Much better."

He chuckles, a rare but breathtaking sound. Then he sets his pen and paper aside on the coffee table and stretches his arms above his head. "Do I lose points against me for not knowing that?"

"Hmmm . . ." I thrum my finger on my bottom lip as I amble across the living room toward him. "I might consider letting you keep all your points for a small fee, of course."

"And what's the fee?" he asks, mildly amused.

I straddle his lap and announce my fee with my actions. He briefly tenses from the contact then relaxes when I tangle my fingers through his hair.

"There. Much better," I whisper. "I don't like you being so far away."

He offers me a small smile. "I wanted to sit by you, but I worried your dad would maybe get mad or something."

"That we were sitting on the couch together?"

"I don't know . . . yeah. I mean, I'm worried maybe they'll figure out we have something going on."

"Have something going on?" I playfully tease. "I'm not sure what you mean. What's going on?"

He stares at me, unimpressed. "I mean our relationship that they don't know about yet."

"Oh, right. I completely forgot about that." I smile innocently at him, and he pinches my side, causing me to yelp. "No fair." I pinch him back, right on his chest.

Tension ripples through his body as he stiffens from my unexpected touch.

"Sorry." I quickly apologize. "I don't know what I was thinking."

"I-it's okay," he stammers through a loud exhale. Then he takes my hand and lines my palm right over his thundering heart. "You just surprised me. That's all . . . You can . . . I'm fine with you touching me on the outside of my shirt. You know that, right?" His off-pitch tone reveals exactly how difficult it is for him to say that.

Touching Ayden is a gift.

One I'm grateful he gives me.

I just wish I could have it all the time.

Every day and night.

On and on and on.

Forever.

I lean forward and place a kiss on his lips. His breathing accelerates as he grasps onto my hips, and I smile to myself, secretly loving that I can make him react like that.

"Maybe we shouldn't do this here," he mutters as I kiss him again. "Your dad's in the next room, and your mom could walk in at any moment."

"Don't worry about them." I rock my hips against his, eliciting a groan from him. "Only stop if you want to stop."

Please, please, don't stop.

Ever, ever, ever.

His protests shift into throaty moans as he deepens the kiss, entangling our tongues, tasting me deeply while his hands travel up and down my sides. His fingers trace each bump of my ribs before drifting down to the hem of my black and purple dress. His fingers tremble as he fiddles with the bottom, something he usually does.

Having more than likely suffered from sexual abuse while being kidnapped, intimacy is complicated with Ayden. Touching me is less of a problem than getting touched himself, but he's always a bit unsettled.

"Do we need to slow down?" I ask, then steal another taste of his lips.

"I don't know." He puts a sliver of space between our mouths, breathing hotly against my lips. "It's getting easier. Sort of. I mean, I don't panic as much, and I feel like I want . . ." He trails off, his eyes glazed over and pupils dilated, as if he's high from the kiss.

High on our kiss.
Dazed by our connection
And the overpowering heat
Of our bodies,
Our souls.
Intoxicated by love.

God, how I wish,

Wish that were the truth.

After searching my eyes, his lips return to mine, and his hand slides underneath my dress, silently answering my question. I fall into his touch, desperately tumbling into a place I once dreamed about but now know exists.

Love.

I'm pretty sure I'm in love with Ayden, but fear has stopped me from telling him, terrified that my declaration will freak him out.

He cups my ass, pushing me closer until our bodies conform. I slide my arms around him then trace my fingers up and down the nape of his neck, kissing him with everything I'm feeling, hoping it'll be enough to get it out of my system.

When his mouth leaves mine, I make a raspy protest, but words get lost as he places tender kisses down my jawline to my neck. He sucks and nips on the flesh, causing my body to swelter with overbearing heat.

"Ah . . . This feels so good," I moan with my head tipped back, clutching onto his shoulders and wishing the moment would never end.

But as soon as the wish surfaces, the front door opens, the alarm goes off, and the moment goes poof. We scramble apart, breathless, our clothes and hair in disarray. I stumble across the room back to the sofa, smoothing my dress back into place. Dropping down on the cushion, I quickly scoop up my sketchpad and pencil right as the alarm gets silenced.

My mother, Fiona, and Everson enter the living room from the foyer while my father comes hurrying in from the hallway.

"What's going on?" he asks as he rushes in. "Why's the alarm going . . . ?" He trails off when he sees my mom. "That was a quick trip."

"Yeah, we just went through the drive-thru." My mother gives a suspicious glance between Ayden and me. "What have you two been up to?"

Shrugging, I press the tip of my pencil against the paper. "Nothing. Just chillin'."

"Sure you were." She exchanges a look with my father, and for a flash of an instant, I wonder if they know exactly what Ayden and I were up to. "Did you check on them at all while I was gone?"

My dad shrugs at her. "Not really, but the alarm was

set so I'd know if they tried to leave."

"I'm not worried about them leaving."

"Then what are you worried about?"

Hello, Captain Oblivious. Even I get what she's worried about.

She presses him with a look, but he still appears lost, either clueless about what my mom's implying or unwilling to accept it.

"I have a few things I've got to take care of," he says to her, backing out of the room. "Meet you upstairs in, like, twenty minutes?"

My mom heaves an exhausted sigh. "All right."

He waggles his eyebrows at her, and then the two of them exchange a look meant only for them to see, even though there's a room full of eyes.

"Wow, way to be obvious, you two," I say to break the awkward silence in the room.

My mother shoots me a dirty look, and I flash her a smirk.

"She's just like you," she tells my dad. "You know that, right?"

"I do." He grins, pleased. "And I'll take that as the

highest compliment." He winks at me before turning and disappearing down the hallway.

My mom brushes her auburn hair off her shoulder then turns to me. "I'm going to go upstairs to take a shower. Try to behave. And have everyone in bed within the next hour."

I give her a salute. "Yes, boss."

She rolls her eyes but smiles before walking off toward the stairway. Moments later, I hear the alarm beep, meaning she set it.

Once all the parentals are out of the room, Fiona, the youngest Gregorys, plops down on the sofa beside Ayden. Kale hurries up to me, hands me a bowl of caramel swirled ice cream, then sits down on the armrest.

"I brought you ice cream." She gives Ayden one of the cups. "I got cookie dough because I know it's your favorite."

Ayden stares at the bowl with his brows knit. "How'd you know it's my favorite?"

Fiona rolls her eyes. "You think you're so mysterious, Ayden, but let me tell you, you kind of aren't." She shovels a spoonful of ice cream into her mouth then flashes him a grin. "You said something about it being your favorite during your birthday."

"Did I?" Ayden wonders, diving into his ice cream. "I don't remember telling anyone that."

"You told Lyric, just like you tell her every other secret of yours." She kicks her feet up onto the coffee table with a sassy smirk on her face.

Ayden and I share an amused look because Fiona is a typical thirteen-year-old—full of rebellion, a sassy attitude, and keeps everyone on their toes.

"Just like you share everything else with her, including your body," she adds with a giggle.

Ayden and my eyes snap wide open, and she erupts in a fit of giggles.

Kale chokes on his ice cream. "Jesus, Fi, where's your filter?"

"I don't share my body with her." Ayden's voice cracks.

Technically, he isn't lying. I haven't touched Ayden anywhere other than on the outside of his clothes. I, however, have been very giving with my body.

"Fiona, why would you say that?" I ask coolly, stirring my ice cream.

She dabs the tears of laughter from her eyes. "Because

it's true. Everyone knows it."

I lick a heap of ice cream off the spoon. "Who's everyone?"

She shrugs indifferently. "Me, Kale, Everson, half the kids at school."

"What about my parents?" I ask her. "And yours? Do they know?"

She shakes her head. "I don't think they know yet. They're pretty oblivious when it comes to these sorts of things."

I kick back on the sofa with my feet propped under me and stuff a bite full of ice cream into my mouth. When our relationship started heating up, Ayden and I agreed it'd be for the best if we kept it a secret for a while. With our families being so tight, we know that the moment they find out, they'll start giving us rules and having expectations. At eighteen-years-old, we want to have a normal relationship without parents getting involved and making everything all awkward.

"I wouldn't get too relaxed if I were you," she remarks. "Sooner or later, they're going to find out, and it'd be better if you guys told them; otherwise, you're going to hurt their feelings. You know how sensitive they can be."

I catch Ayden's gaze. "She's probably right."

He squirms uncomfortably. "Yeah, maybe." He shoves a bite of ice cream into his mouth and stares at the fireplace, lost in thought.

I open my mouth to ask him if everything's okay, but Kale speaks first. "Ayden, could you help me with something?" he asks, quickly hopping to his feet.

Ayden tears his gaze off the fireplace and blinks up at him. "What's up?"

Kale scratches his nose, appearing as uneasy as Ayden. "Can we talk about it upstairs in the guest room?" His gaze skims over Fiona and me. "In private."

"Sure." Ayden flicks a glance in my direction before he rises to his feet, looking as squirrely as the first day we met. "I'll see you in the morning."

I frown after he hurries out of the room like it's on fire. "I wonder what that's about."

"Kale has a crush on this girl at school," Fiona explains, misinterpreting what I meant. "But, since he's a weirdo, he needs Ayden's help trying to get this girl's attention. I don't know why he asked Ayden, though. He's just as much of a weirdo as Kale." She gives an elongated pause. “We all kind of are.” Her eyes sparkle with mischief as they land on me. “That includes you, too, you know. You’re seriously as insane as the rest of us.”

“I never claimed to be sane.” I jab the spoon at the ice cream, still stuck on why Ayden seemed all squiggly. “Besides, normal is so overrated. Trust me. I have a few friends who are normal, and I’d rather poke my eye out than live their lives of going off to college as soon as I graduate, getting a normal job, and eventually starting a family.”

With senior year nearing the end, it’s all everyone talks about anymore. Going off to college to pursue a degree that will give them an average job with stable pay.

“You don’t plan on going to college?”

“No. At least, not until I see what I can do with my music career.”

“Isn’t that sort of risky?”

“Yeah.” I balance the bowl on the armrest. “But I’d risk my sanity if I didn’t at least try.”

“Does your mom and dad know about this?” She sets the cup of ice cream on her knee and starts side-braiding her long, brown hair.

“I’ve mentioned it a couple of times,” I tell her. “They’re a little bit more hesitant than I am that it’ll all work out."

"Figures. Parents so don't understand dreams." She secures the braid with an elastic.

"What's with the third degree, anyway? You're thirteen. Aren't you supposed to be worrying about crushes and makeup and stuff like that?"

"I do worry about that stuff, but as an aspiring artist, I also worry about my art and whether or not becoming an artist is in my future."

"I'm sure it is." I stand up with my sketchbook in my hand. "Your sketches are amazing."

"So are yours and your mother's." She collects the cup off her lap and hops to her feet, tugging at the hem of her yellow dress. "Can I see what you're drawing?"

I hesitate. The detailed drawing of Ayden feels very private and intimate, but then I realize it doesn't really matter since she already knows about our relationship.

"What the hell." I hold out my sketchpad for her to see.

She examines it closely, and a smile spans across her face. "It looks so much like him it's crazy."

I grin at her approval, tuck the sketchpad under my arm, and motion at her as I head for the stairs. "Come on.

Let's go get ready for bed, and then I'll let you look at more of them."

She skips after me. "Thanks, Lyric. You're the best neighbor-who's-like-a-sister ever."

"Yeah, yeah," I start up the stairway, "you say that now, but I'm sure you'll change your mind like you do every other day."

She giggles. "Yeah, you're probably right."

After we're in our pajamas, we get situated in my room. Since we only have one guestroom in my house, Ayden and Kale are staying in it, so Fiona is camping out on my floor in a sleeping bag. The lights are off, but she uses her phone as a flashlight while she flips through my sketchpad.

"There's so many pictures of Ayden." She turns another page. "Lyric?"

"Yeah?" I answer sleepily.

"Do you love him?"

"Love who?" I yawn, already half asleep.

"Ayden."

I freeze mid-yawn and open my mouth to say no, but the lie won't leave my lips.

"It's okay," she reassures me, "I won't tell anyone."

I smile to myself as I roll over and close my eyes. I fall asleep to the sound of turning pages and my mind filled with a thousand lyrics.

So soft are his lips,

Like rose petals and velvet.

The taste of him is indescribable.

The feel of his body almost unbearable.

When he kisses me, I swear I'm dying.

Out of air, body aching, knees shaking.

More, more, more,

Always craving more.

Love, it's like an addiction,

Consuming the mind.

Love, love, love.

I'm so in love with him.

Chapter 4

Lyric

I'm woken up in the dead of sleep by violent shaking. Still half stuck in dreamland, at first I think it's an earth-quake, but as my eyes adjust to the night, I realize it's Fiona.

"Lyric, wake up." She gives my shoulder another shake.

"What's wrong?" I sit up, rub my eyes, and then glance at the clock. "Dude, it's only four o'clock in the morning. What the hell, Fiona?"

"It's Ayden," she says, her eyes wild with panic. "He's in trouble."

Just like that, I'm wide awake, like my body has been hotwired.

"What's wrong?" I fling the blankets off my body and spring from the bed.

"I had a dream about him," she whispers, hugging her

arms around herself.

I instantly relax. "I'm sorry you had a nightmare, but seriously, you can't wake me up this early." I'm not a morning person at all.

"It wasn't a nightmare," she huffs in frustration, stomping her foot on the floor. "It really happened."

I sink down on the edge of my bed, yawning. "What happened?"

"Ayden . . . I was dreaming about him sleepwalking outside, and then the dream came true." Pale moonlight trickles through the window and highlights the fear in her expression.

"I know nightmares can be scary," I say in the most sympathetic voice I can muster at this early of an hour, "but you have to remember that they're just that—nightmares."

"It wasn't a nightmare." She marches up to the window and points at something outside. "If you don't believe me, then take a look for yourself."

My heart immediately starts pumping blood through my body at an alarming rate. I rise to my feet, pad over to the window, and peer down at the ground. At first, all I see is nightfall covering the neighborhood. But as I strain my vision, I spot a figure next door, standing out on the Gregory's front yard.

No, not Ayden. He's not supposed to leave the house and definitely not in the middle of the night.

"Ayden . . ." I whirl to Fiona. "Go wake up my mom." I run out of my room, down the stairs, and cringe when I realize the front door is wide open, and the alarm has been turned off.

Ayden knows the code, so I'm guessing he did it somehow while he's sleepwalking.

What the hell?

Even though it's April, the cement is cold against my bare feet as I race down the driveway and around the fence dividing our yards. The road is dimly lit by lampposts that offer just enough light so I'm not running around blind.

As I approach him, my pulse soars. Wide-eyed and out of it, his lips are moving as he mutters under his breath. I've found Ayden sleepwalking before, and like the first time, he's talking about stuff I don't understand.

"We're not going to let you out that easy," he mutters, staring dazedly at a car on the corner of the road. "No one leaves us. Ever."

I struggle over what to do. I know better than to wake

him up; otherwise, he might flip out. But I need to get him back into the house somehow.

I reach out to touch his arm, hoping to subtly guide him back without waking him, when he turns his head and looks at me.

"We're going to come for you," he mutters. "And you're going to wish you never escaped . . ." He blinks his eyes, and then his lips part. "What the hell?" In a panic, he glances around at the houses. "Where the hell am I . . . ? How did I . . . ?" His enlarged eyes lock on me. "I don't . . ."

Shit. He's waking up and panicking.

"It's okay." I cautiously inch toward him with my arms open, preparing to hug him, but he skitters away from me with his hands out in front of him.

"How the fuck did I get out here?" he demands in a harsh voice, his eyes watering up as he gasps for air. "I don't understand."

I keep my hands in front of me while stepping toward him. "You were sleepwalking, I think. But it's okay. Everything's okay."

He clenches his hands into fists and sucks in a breath

to fight back the tears, but a few escape and cascade down his cheeks. "I'm so sick of this. I feel like I'm losing my goddamn mind."

"I know, but it's going to be okay." I have no idea what else to say. No clue what to do. I feel so helpless at the moment.

"I'm so sorry." His head slumps forward as he starts to cry.

"You have nothing to be sorry about." I loop my arm around his back and steer him toward my house. "Let's get you inside."

Nodding, his arms wraps around my waist. We hike around the fence, up the driveway, and to the front porch. I only let him go to shut the front door, but freeze when I notice the car on the corner that Ayden was staring at now has the headlights on.

I watch as it flips a U-turn and peels off down the street. With everything that has been happening, I wonder if it isn't a coincidence that the car drives off the moment we head back inside. Could it be someone stalking Ayden again?

"Lyric, what's going on?" My mother's voice floats over my shoulder.

I lock the door then turn around. She has on a robe, her hair is a tangled mess, and her tired eyes are bouncing back and forth between Fiona, Ayden, and me.

I hurry and explain what happened, making sure to include the car. She tells me not to worry, that it was probably one of the neighbors heading off to work, but her eyes show her concern.

“Let’s all get back to bed, and we can talk it about in the morning, okay? When Lila and Ethan get home,” my mom says, ushering us toward the stairs. “I can’t believe you managed to turn the alarm off in your sleep,” she mutters quietly.

“I’m sorry,” Ayden apologizes as we ascend the stairs. “I don’t know how I did it, either.”

“Don’t be sorry,” my mother says from behind us. “This isn’t your fault, sweetie.”

Ayden bites down on his lip, not saying anything else.

“Are you okay?” I whisper to him.

“I don’t know,” he mumbles under his breath, loud enough that only I can hear.

I graze my fingers along his arm. “I’m here if you want to talk about it in the morning.”

He nods, and then we part ways at the top of the stairway. Fiona follows me into my room and slides back into the sleeping bag while I climb into bed.

By the time I pull the covers over me, the sun is kissing the edges of San Diego and glowing across the sky, casting rays of light into my room. Restless, I stay awake to write, silently expressing what I can't say aloud, allowing myself to get lost in my words.

"Lyric, I'm scared," Fiona says so abruptly I jump and chuck the pen I'm holding like I'm some sort of spastic ninja.

"Jesus, I thought you were sleeping." I set down my journal, lean over to the side, and peer down at her. "You don't need to be scared. Ayden's fine."

"That's not what I'm scared about." She tugs the sleeping bag up higher as she gazes up at the ceiling. "I'm scared I'll have more nightmares if I shut my eyes."

"You said you dreamed that Ayden was sleepwalking?"

"Sort of," she replies vaguely. "Then, when I woke up, I saw him out on the front lawn."

This isn't the first time she has said something strange to me. There was an incident when Ayden was sleepwalking and screaming, and Fiona said she felt his scream, whatever that means.

"Does this kind of stuff happen to you a lot? I mean, do you dream about things that happen?"

"I don't dream it . . . I feel it happen." With her eyes opened so wide, she looks utterly horrified. She abruptly bolts upright and snatches hold of my hand in desperation. "You can't tell anyone that. Promise me, Lyric." When I don't agree right away, she tightens her hold on my hand. "This is important. I need it to stay a secret, just like you need the fact that you're dating Ayden to stay a secret."

I have no idea what's going on. If she's blackmailing me. If she's crazy. If I'm crazy because I kind of believe her.

"All right, I promise," I say with reluctance. "Just as long as you keep quiet about me and Ayden."

"I will." She releases her grasp on my hand and lies back down on the floor. "Thanks, Lyric." She rolls over on her side, and a minute later, she's fast asleep, breathing softly.

Wigged out by the last few hours of events, I grab another pen from my nightstand drawer and return to my journal to write. My thoughts drift from what Fiona told me to what happened with Ayden. The pen floats fluidly across the paper, pouring out my soul and the deepest fears I don't dare utter aloud.

How do I save him
When the world has so much control?
Spinning through life, a turbulent force,
Sucking him down into a dark hole.
Sunlight spills upon me,
Drowns me in warmth.
I outrun it for as long as I can.
He's falling into the dark, begging to be saved,
Pleading for me to save him.
I reach for him,
But the sunlight devours me
And burns my hands,
Singeing me to dust.

Chapter 5

Ayden

Last night was going okay until Lyric mentioned that we'd eventually have to tell our parents we're dating. I never really thought about it too much, but once she pointed it out, I realized she was right. One day, they'll find out about us, and I'll have to face my unworthiness. Deep down, I've always known her parents weren't going to be thrilled about the messed up guy next door dating their cheery, upbeat daughter. I was ruined the moment I was chained up in that house. Those days spent locked under that roof changed me, fucked me up, poisoned my skin with marks that will never go away.

To top off the declining night, I ended up sleepwalking to the front lawn, which was not only terrifying as hell, but also extremely dangerous, all things considering.

I have no memory of what happened until the point

when Lyric woke me up, yet the moment Lila and Ethan return home the next afternoon, they expect me to recount the details to them.

After Kale, Everson, and Fiona are set up at the table, doing their homework, the three of us sit down in the living room with cups of coffee and cookies because Lila believes sugar eases tense situations.

"I really can't tell you too much about what happened." I pick at a loose thread in the knee of my jeans. "All I can remember is waking up and seeing Lyric."

Lyric, poor Lyric.
Worried out of her mind
As she stared into my eyes
And tried to read what was hidden in my
mind.
What would she see if she broke through the
lock?
What I witnessed all those days I was
trapped in the dark?
I wish she never had to see that side of me.
Wish. Wish. Wish.
Wish I could be the guy she deserves,
The one who touches her with everything,

Gives her everything,

Could give her undying love.

"What about the car?" Lila brings the brim of a coffee mug to her mouth and sips. She's been pretending to be calm, but under the surface, I can tell she's frightened about the ordeal.

"I didn't really notice it." I stuff the rest of the cookie into my mouth then wipe my hands off. "Lyric did."

"Lyric said you were staring at it." Ethan threads his fingers through Lila's to comfort her. "And then it drove away the moment you got into the house."

"If that's what she said, then I'm sure it happened that way." I lift my shoulder and shrug, unsure of what they want me to say. "I swear, if I knew more, I'd tell you, but I'm just as confused as you." And terrified out of my mind.

I'll never admit that aloud, though, because then they'll only worry about me more.

I've lived with the Gregorys for over two years now, and they're some of the nicest people I've ever met. Always wanting to keep me safe. Always trying to protect me.

"We know you'd tell us if you could remember," Lila says, setting the cup of coffee down on the table. "I just think what we really want to make sure of is that you're okay. I know it's got to be hard, being stalked by these people and always worrying if . . ." She smashes her lips together as she emotionally tears up.

The clock ticks in the background. Out the window, the sun is shining across the clear blue sky, cars zip up and down the street. A neighbor is shouting at a dog, and a lady with bright red hair is strolling down the sidewalk. Her hair reminds me of blood and almost throws me back into a memory of when I ran into that house. I almost let the images through, because I want to help my sister, want to remember who the people were that took us. But my body constricts, forcing the images to fade away.

"I'm not sure what you want me to say other than I'm fine." I blink my attention away from the window, pick up my cup of coffee, and gulp down the hot drink.

"Okay." Lila casts a glance at Ethan. "Still, it has to be really, really stressful, especially when we don't know if they're going to show up again."

She seems fairly adamant about pointing out the danger of the situation, and I'm not sure why. She knows I understand, so there has to be some other reason.

"Ethan and I worry about you," she continues. "After

the note and the car being out there last night, we think it might be a good idea if you aren't alone very much."

"Haven't I been doing that already?" I ask. "Especially after getting that note the other day and then talking to the detective."

"Yes, but . . ." She glances at Ethan again. "We just want to make sure you understand the importance of you following the rules and being safe."

"Yeah, I understand the rules. Have for a while." I glance back and forth between them. "Is there something you aren't telling me?"

It wouldn't be the first time they've kept stuff from me in order to try to protect me from the harsh reality.

"We're not keeping anything from you." Ethan leans forward in the seat and rests his elbows on his knees. "We just want to make sure you're being safe, and you're taking care of yourself mentally. We think you've been a little too quiet these last couple of months."

"I've always been quiet." *Where are they going with this?*

"We know that, but it seems like, ever since you found out about your sister, you've been even quieter."

"We just want you to know how sorry we are that this is happening," Lila adds, her eyes welled up with tears. "I know it's got to be hard, especially after what happened to your brother."

I flex my fingers as my hands begin to tremble.

My brother, gone forever.

Gone, gone, gone.

Just like my sister might be.

After we all miraculously made it out of the house alive, only one of us might survive.

Or maybe none, depending on the outcome.

It isn't like I haven't ever thought about it—that the Soulless Mileas could get ahold of me again—I've worried about it every hour of every day for the last four years. The note increased the fear, though, and made the idea very re-al.

"We just want you to know that we're here for you if you ever need anything." Lila stands up, crosses the room, and takes a seat beside me. "We love you, Ayden. If you need anything at all, you can let us know, and we'll do whatever's in our power to make it happen."

It's a nice offer, but what I want isn't in their power—a normal life with my sister and without the painful reminder of the past branded on my flesh.

Then a couple of ideas strike me from out of nowhere, ideas I've contemplated before but have been too afraid to ask.

"There actually might a couple of things you can do for me." I sit up straighter in the chair. "Could you ask the detective if I can read the letter my sister wrote? I want to know what's on there."

Lila's expression fills with remorse. "I'm not sure they'll agree to that, seeing as how it's evidence." She places a hand on my back, a motherly gesture, but still, the contact causes me to tense.

"Could you at least ask?" I ask, one step away from begging her. "It can't hurt to ask, right? And maybe it could help me figure out what I'm getting into since she wrote the note right after she was kidnapped."

"If that's what you need, then I guess I can ask." A deep frown etches her face, and worry lines crease the corners of her eyes.

Knowing Lila, she's probably worried how I'll react to reading the letter, hence the hesitancy. It isn't for her to decide, though. I *need* to know what's in the note my sister was forced to write and mail to the police while she's being held captive somewhere by people who are skeletons of human beings and once tried to drain our souls dry.

"Thanks." I scratch at my side, preparing to ask my next question. "I also want to get the tattoo on my side covered up . . . the one they put on me."

It's a big step just asking for it, but I've wanted the tattoo removed forever. The only thing stopping me has been my fear of being touched during the inking and of tumbling into a memory. I want to believe I have the hidden strength to do it, though.

Lila glances at Ethan. "What do you think?"

"I actually like the idea of getting rid of it." He digs his phone from his pocket. "I have a buddy who owns a tattoo parlor down by where I work. He does good work. I could take you in to see what it would take to get it covered up."

"Thanks. That'd be great."

I know it won't solve my problems, but the idea of having the tattoo gone gives me the strangest sense of peace.

A taste of freedom

From the bleeding ink

Staining my skin

Like the blood on their hands.

Gone, gone, gone,

The ink is fading away.

Maybe after it's erased,

I can finally feel like I was actually saved.

After Lila and Ethan agree to my requests, I collect the car keys to head to my therapy appointment.

"You're just going straight there, right?" Lila checks while walking me to the door.

I shake my head as I grab my jacket from the coatrack. "Yeah, I don't have band practice tonight." Throwing a wave over my shoulder, I open the door and step outside beneath the clouds.

"You'll call me when you get there, right?" Lila asks, following me outside. "And text the therapist to come walk you in if no one's around?"

"Yeah, I know the drill." I stop at the end of the walk-way, studying her. She has her arms folded tightly around her, and her gaze is continuously inspecting the houses across the street. *Odd.* "Is everything okay?"

"Of course." She smiles stiffly. "I was just making sure that car wasn't out here. Lyric said it was a black, newer model, right?"

"I think so." I eye her warily, not believing her story. "But you do realize that description fits every other car in this neighborhood."

She sighs. "I know. I really wish she could have gotten a better look at it."

Raindrops start to fall from the sky, and I pull my hood over my head. "It could have been someone going to work."

"Yeah, it could have," she replies, seeming doubtful. Her eyes rise to the stormy sky, and she shields her hair from the rain with her arm. "Anyway, you get going. I'm going to be here all day, so if you need anything at all, then call."

Nodding, I jog up the driveway toward the black, newer BMW, which kind of proves my point about the car. With everything that's happened, though, I can't blame them for being concerned. I just wish I wasn't such a burden, always causing stress and worry.

Lila remains on the front porch, watching me back onto the road and steer toward the main street.

I make the drive toward the therapist's office across town with the radio up, listening to one of the playlists Lyric made for me. Being in the car alone always makes me edgy, and I'm always checking in my rearview mirror for some sign someone is tailing me.

Today, I swear a massive maroon SUV with tinted windows matches my every turn and lane change. But right as I start to panic, the vehicle veers down a side road.

Breathing easily, I flip on the blinker at the next road and take a right, driving into a rundown neighborhood located a few miles away from my therapist's office.

A light drizzle of rain sprinkles from the clouds as I park the car in front of the house that was the last address listed for Sadie.

The house is boarded up and painted with jagged circular symbols that match the tattoo on my ribs. The home resembles most of the surrounding structures on the street, so the entire area is extremely creepy. In a strange way, the place reminds me of the home I grew up in and how damn lucky I am to be living where I am now.

I know it isn't the best thing to be here, but I can't help myself. Something about the place terrifies me yet draws me to it.

I've been making the detour for the last month. Every

time I stop by, I contemplate going inside and looking around in the hope that I get a better understanding of what Sadie went through while she was living here. But I've never gotten the balls to even get out of the car.

I remain in the car, staring at the peeling paint, wondering if it was put there after Sadie was kidnapped or if they did it beforehand. The detective said our cases are similar, and that they stalked her first before taking her, but I still don't know exactly how it happened.

I don't know

Anything

About her

Other than my heart aches for her.

A year younger than me, Sadie should be a junior in high school, having fun, going to parties like I used to before I got put on lockdown. I haven't seen her since we were removed from that house four years ago, and I don't know what her life has been like since then. Looking at the homes around me, I'm guessing it hasn't been great.

I gawk at the house for ten minutes straight before I put the car in drive and start to pull away.

"I promise I won't let anything happen to you," I whisper to Sadie from across the room.

"How? You're tied up, too," she cries through the darkness, her voice weak.

Chains, chains, chains bite at my flesh.

Peel back the skin, reveal what's inside.

Look at me raw, see the truth in my eyes.

"I don't know how, but I will, Sadie. I swear."

Broken promises,

Cracked and ruptured.

Left behind,

Like dust on the floor.

I'm sorry I lied.

I slam on the brakes and strangle the steering wheel as the memory crawls under my skin. Fueled with the need to see what's hidden in the house, to understand just how badly I let my sister down, I shove the car back into park, fling the door open, and climb out.

Raindrops splatter across my face and drip from my hair as I hike up the lopsided driveway. When I reach the side door of the house, I glance around to make sure no one is watching me before opening it.

The smell of mold and rot engulfs my nostrils as I step over the threshold and inside what looks like a kitchen. The floorboards groan under my boots as I inch my way into the darkness.

Sticking my hand into my pocket, I remove my phone and turn on the flashlight app to get a better look around.

The cupboards are hanging crooked on the walls, the countertops are torn up, and shards of glass cover the floor.

I carefully maneuver my way through the kitchen and into the living room, the atmosphere growing darker as the outside world slips away from me. To my right is a stair-way, but most of the steps are missing. I veer in the opposite direction toward a closed door tucked behind a raised wall. Painted across the wall are words that are way too familiar: *Running away is like running in circles. You can't escape once we've found your soul, and soon, you'll end up back in the same place.*

A cold shiver courses through me. I heard those words whispered during the weeks I was trapped.

Panicking, I turn away, but stop mid-turn.

No. I need to go through with this.

Wheeling back around, I inch toward the door, notic-ing an *S* carved in the wood right above the doorknob.

No, not Sadie.

My phone buzzes a few times, but I ignore it, needing

to go through with this. I wrap my fingers around the metal knob and, with a deep breath, push open the door.

The stench of the room smothers the air from my lungs, heavy and weighted like death. I cough, covering my mouth with my arm as I glance around the small room with caved in walls and a rotting floor. In the middle of the mess is the metal frame of a bed. I can almost picture my sister sitting on it day in and day out, waiting to be saved, but no one ever shows up, and soon she's taken away to a far worse life than even this.

Tears sting my eyes. I know it isn't a memory, but thinking about what she must have gone through—is still going through—aches deep inside me like searing hot metal against my bones.

As I veer toward a panic attack, I spin on my heels and rush out of the house. By the time I burst back into the rain, I'm quivering from head to toe as fear pulsates through me. I run down the driveway toward my car, needing to get the hell out of here. Rain pours from the sky and soaks through my clothes as my boots splash through the puddles.

"Excuse me. Do you live here?" A woman wearing a bright red raincoat with the hood pulled over her head is suddenly at the end of the driveway.

I slam to a stop and hurry and wipe my eyes with my sleeve, trying to catch my breath. “No . . . I was just . . . I knocked on the door, but no one answered,” I lie, unsure of what else to say.

She glances at the home then at me. “You know it’s vacant, right?”

“I figured that out, yes.” As casually as I can, I move to the right to swing around her, knowing if I stand near that house for too long, I’ll lose my shit.

“Didn’t the boarded up windows and spray paint kind of give that away?” she asks, sidestepping and blocking my path.

Red flags pop up everywhere.

My eyelashes flutter against the rainstorm as I skim her over. She’s medium height, a little on the thin side, and is wearing black rain boots. Her hood is pulled so low I can hardly see her face, but her voice sounds gruff, like a heavy smoker.

Do I know that voice? Or am I just being paranoid?

Her hair isn’t red like blood, red like the woman who always wanted to touch me. That’s the only sense of comfort I have at the moment, but hair dye can easily fix that.

I duck my head to get a better look at her, but she steps back, stuffing her hands into her pockets.

"You better be careful. This place isn't safe." She spins on her heels and runs down the sidewalk away from me.

"Hey!" I call out, hurrying after her.

I don't know why, but I have this crazy feeling that she might know something.

She picks up her speed as she nears the end of the block. I bring my pace from a jog to a sprint as she makes a left and disappears behind a fence. By the time I reach the corner, she's gone.

"Shit!" I curse, kicking a street sign.

"Ayden."

I freeze then turn around, shielding my eyes as I squint through the rain at Lila who's standing a few feet away from me, wearing her coat and carrying an umbrella.

"I . . . Why are you . . . ?" I look around the street and spot a maroon SUV parked at the entrance of the neighborhood, the same car I thought was following me. "What's going on?"

"Shouldn't I be asking you the same question?" She shakes her head with dismay. "Get in the car. We need to talk."

I look back in the direction the woman vanished. "There was someone here, talking to me. It seemed like she was warning me about something."

Lila leans forward and peers down the street while positioning the umbrella over both of our heads.

"They're not there anymore," I explain. "But it was a woman, and—I don't know—I have a bad feeling about her."

She frowns as she looks back at me. "This entire place is one bad feeling. Now get in the car so you can explain to me what the hell you were thinking coming here."

The walk back to the car is painfully slow and quiet. By the time we climb inside, the SUV is pulling away, and the rain has slowed down.

"Who is that?" I ask, pointing at the vehicle.

"That was an undercover detective," she says, slamming the car door.

"What?" Suddenly, their little not-being-alone speech makes much more sense. "Why is he following me?"

"Well, for starters, we want to make sure you're safe. And secondly, because Dr. Gardingdale informed us that you've been late to the last eight sessions."

"You could have just asked me what I was doing."

She elevates her brows at me accusingly. "Every time we ask you about anything, you tell us you're fine. Plus, you tracked down this place"—she nods her head at the house—"all by yourself. You searched for your sister's address for months, and Lyric was the only one you ever told. So, how could I possibly know you'd tell us the truth if I asked?"

Okay, she has a point.

"We needed to find out where you were going since you won't ever tell us anything." She tosses the umbrella into the backseat, and then her eyes narrow at me. "I hate being this kind of mom—the one who gets angry at her children—but seriously, what the hell were you thinking, coming here by yourself?"

"The police investigated this place after Sadie was taken," I remind her as I rev up the engine and flip on the wipers. "They didn't find anything suspicious other than the paint on the outside and inside."

"Other than the paint." She gapes at me. "Ayden, that paint all over the house matches that mark on your side, the one put on you against your will. That's not a little thing."

"I know." I lose my voice as guilt creeps up inside me for upsetting her. "But I just wanted to see for myself."

Her expression slightly softens. "I understand that you want to know what's going on—we all do—but you can't go around looking for stuff on your own. Not after what's been going on and that note . . ." She trails off, shaking her head.

I flop my head back against the headrest. "I get that I fucked up, but I feel like I'm losing my damn mind. Every day, I wake up worried something's going to happen to me. Or worse, the police will knock on our door again, only this time, they'll be there to tell me my sister's been found dead."

She's quiet for a while, probably trying to figure out what the hell to say to my out of the blue confession.

"I get that it's hard." She gently places a hand on my arm, and for once, I don't flinch. "But wandering off by yourself isn't going to help. You need to let the police do their job and focus on yourself and getting better. Talking like this—telling me how you feel—that's a start. I've never heard you be so open."

"I think I'm just getting tired of keeping everything locked in all the time." I shut my eyes. "It's hard just to focus on myself when it feels like anyone could be them. Like that woman I just saw."

"What did she say to you exactly?" she asks, cranking up the heat. I recap the last five minutes to her, and she frowns when I'm finished.

"Honestly, I'm not that worried. This area is very sketchy, and it could have easily been a nervous drug dealer or something. But I'll go let the detective know about her, and maybe they can track her down."

I draw the seatbelt strap over my shoulder. "How long have I been followed?"

"Only since the note."

"How long am I going to be followed?"

"Until we know you're safe." She nods as she sticks her hand into her coat pocket and retrieves her phone. "Besides, they're hoping the next time they try to do something, they'll catch them in the act."

"So, they're watching me all the time."

"For the most part." She gives me a sidelong glance. "So no more running off to dangerous places." She reaches for the door handle. "Now, go straight to your appointment and then home. Nowhere else. Don't go looking for that woman. Let the police handle it."

"All right," I reply, because I don't really have any other choice.

"Thank you for making this easy." She hops out into the now sprinkling rain.

"Wait. How did you get here?" I ask, leaning over the console.

"The detective called me the moment he figured out where you were going." She lowers her head to look at me. "When I got the call, I hopped in my car and drove as crazy as Ella to get here."

"Where's your car?"

She points diagonally across the street, and I easily spot the back end of her silver Mercedes.

"Oh." Through the rain and the distraction of the woman, I must have somehow missed the obvious.

"I'll see you in about an hour and a half." She closes the door, and just like that, our conversation ends.

As I make the short drive to therapy with the SUV tailing me, I feel like I've been put on probation. Having come from a home where, most of the time, my siblings and I ran wild, I feel strangely okay that. For the first time in a long time, I feel kind of safe.

Ten minutes later, I enter the office where my therapy sessions take place. The rain has let up by the time I walk in, and sunlight sneaks through the clouds and glimmers through the windows.

"Hey, Ayden, how have you been?" Dr. Gardingdale greets without looking up from the filing cabinet he's sifting through.

"Good." I drop down in the chair across from his desk.

He glances up at me. "You don't sound good." He glides the filing cabinet drawer shut, pulls out a chair, and then sits down. "Is something wrong?"

Out of habit, I shake my head, but words slip out of my mouth on their own. "Did you tell Lila I was showing up late to sessions?"

"I did," he answers shamelessly. "I was concerned that you might be doing something that could harm your well-being."

"Why would you figure that?"

"Because of something you said at your last appointment."

"What did I say exactly?"

"That you were thinking about going and looking for

your sister yourself."

"I said that?" Why can't I remember that?

"You were under when you said it," he explains, checking the time on the wall clock. "It was during an amnesia therapy session."

I attempt to remember, but come up blank. "Why didn't you tell me?"

"Because you were upset when you woke up." He tugs on his red and blue striped tie, loosening it. "It was the session where you—"

"Cried," I finish for him.

I cringe at the faint memory of me waking up to the branding iron. The pain was unbearable. I could still feel it when I woke up.

"I didn't want to upset you, but I thought I needed to tell your mother about what happened and about being late to sessions." He pauses, giving me an opening to explain where I've been.

"I think maybe I should reconsider that slip I signed, giving you permission to discuss certain things with the Gregorys."

"Is that what you really want?"

I hesitate then shake my head. "No, not really. They

don't deserve to worry like that."

"I think that's a wise choice." His phone buzzes, and he silences it without looking at it. "So, is there anything else bothering you? Maybe at home? Or at school?" His light questions are his way of easing into the darker stuff, which always comes later in the hour.

"No . . . not exactly . . ." I trail off, uncertain how much talking I want to do today. It's been such a stressful day already. "Nothing's really wrong at home or school."

It's not as easy as it sounds
To confess my darkest worries,
My fears of who I am,
My fear of never being good enough.

He slips on his glasses. "Remember, I can't help you unless I know what the problem is." When I still don't answer, he adds, "Do you want to talk about your sister? I don't usually like to dive into the complicated stuff, but if you need us to, we can. I know what's going on with her has to be stressful. Plus, you've been putting a lot of pressure on yourself with this amnesia therapy because of what's happened to her."

I wipe my sweaty palms on my jeans. "That's not what

I was going to say . . . but I do worry about her. All the time, actually. I even went to that address she used to live at . . . That's why I've been late."

Shock flickers across his face, but he keeps himself professionally composed, his voice remaining even. "Can I ask why you've been going there?"

I shrug. "I was curious where she lived and what her life was like up until she was taken. Plus, in this weird way, it made me feel close to her." I only realize the truth when the words leave my lips.

Deep down, I knew going in that house wouldn't help find Sadie. It was the last place she lived, the last place she might have had a life.

"That's understandable," he says. "It has to be hard on you having not seen her for years, only to find out she's been kidnapped."

"I feel like I hardly got to know her. I was fourteen when we were taken, and she was only thirteen. My older brother was almost sixteen, but still, it seems like such a short amount of time . . . time I'll never get back. And, with my brother, I'll never have a chance to get any more time at all." I force down the lump in my throat.

"I've been dreaming about her a lot . . . Sadie. She's in

a house on this hill, and she's tied up and hurt. I can hear her, but . . . I can't help her. All I want to do is help her, and I feel like, if I can just see what's around the house, then I'll be able to find her. But I never have the dream long enough for me to figure out the exact location."

"Are you sure it's a dream? Perhaps it's a memory."

"I honestly have no fucking idea anymore. Sometimes, it's hard to tell what's really happened and what's a nightmare. Sometimes, I feel like my mind gets all jumbled because it's overthinking too much, if that makes any sense."

Lightning booms from outside, causing me to jump. Out the window, the clouds have rolled in again, blocking the sunlight from the earth.

His forehead creases. "I know you're not going to be happy about this, but I've been considering maybe having you take a break from the amnesia therapy."

"What?" I jolt upright in my seat. "No, I can't do that. Please, don't make me do that."

He offers me a sympathetic look. "Ayden, I'm sorry to say this, because I know you want to help find your sister, but I think we might be putting too much pressure on you, and the brain doesn't do well with stress."

He scoots his chair forward and crosses his arms on his desk. "It was stress and the pain from the situation that made you forget to begin with. Perhaps a little break might be beneficial and might actually help you have an easier time remembering, if that makes sense."

"I don't want to stop the therapy yet, not when my memories are starting to surface on their own." I shift my weight in the chair. "I've actually been thinking a lot about that experimental therapy you told me about, the one Lila doesn't want me to do. I'm eighteen now, though, so doesn't that mean I technically don't need her permission?"

"Legally, you don't need the permission from a guardian, but I wouldn't advise it. Like I said, your brain needs rest." He removes his glasses and cleans the lenses with a rag he fishes from a drawer beside him. "I'm not saying we're going to stop forever. We can go back to the therapy in time."

"My sister doesn't have time," I croak, my emotions thick in my throat.

"Finding your sister isn't solely your job. The police are doing everything in their power to find her."

"The longer she's gone, the less likely she's . . ." My

chest aches just thinking about it, deep wounds hidden beneath the scars.

There were so many scars on all of us when we were pulled out of that house. So many scars showing just how truly evil they were.

"I think we need to start working on some relaxation exercises," he says as he watches me fight to get oxygen into my lungs.

He puts his glasses back on, collects a pen and notebook from the drawer, and then stares at me for the longest time before asking, "Can I ask what you were going to say to start with? I asked you what's wrong when you walked in, but we never made it to what you were going to say."

I gradually inhale then exhale before I can speak. "I was going to say what's been bothering me is . . . Lyric."

"The girl you've been seeing?"

"Yeah. We've actually been dating in secret."

"Why do you feel the need to keep it a secret?" he asks, jotting something down in the notebook.

"We've been saying it's because our parents are really close, and if we told them, they'd start setting all these rules, but . . ." I sketch the scars on the back of my hand, faint white lines put there by fingernails.

"But what?" he treads cautiously. "Remember, in order for me to help you work through the problem, you have to discuss it with me."

A deafening breath escapes my lips. "I'm starting to realize my reason is a bit different than hers."

"How so?"

"I don't know . . . I think I'm just worried about what's going to happen when her parents find out. Lyric . . . She's so happy and full of life. She can make anyone laugh, and everyone loves her. Me,"—I internally cringe—"well, I'm not like that at all."

He writes down a few more notes. "So, you think you don't fit well with her?"

"No, I think she's—that I'm—" I rub my hand down my face, releasing a trapped a breath. "Look, I know I'm not good enough for her."

His hand stops moving across the paper as he peers up. "And what does Lyric say about how you feel?"

"I haven't told her, but if I did, she'd tell me I'm wrong, because that's the kind of person she is."

Silence stretches between us as he slides the notebook aside and overlaps his hands on his desk. "Can I ask why you feel unworthy?"

"Because she's too good for me," I reply with a shrug. "I thought that was pretty clear."

"I think it's only clear to yourself," he explains, meticulously assessing my expression. "I think that, perhaps, because of the verbal abuse with your birth mother and with the trauma you endured in your past, your self-perception is a little distorted."

"I think my past is part of the reason I'm not good enough for her," I disagree with him. "I think I have this dark, fucked-up past that's made me a fucked-up person who doesn't deserve to be with someone who's so happy and good. God, I can barely let her touch me without freaking out. " The truth slips out of me like venom. My breath turns ragged, and my heartbeat skyrockets. "And, if we do make it too far with the physical stuff, I have to battle down this ugly, wrong feeling inside me. I don't want to be this way, though. I wish I could change it . . . just get past it."

"Our past doesn't shape who we are, and as for the not being able to withstand physical contact, that's perfectly understandable considering what happened to you. I know we haven't outright talked about the abuse you went through, but I think maybe, when you're ready, we should start discussing it."

"But how can I discuss something I'm not positive ever happened? I just assume it did because of how I feel inside and through bits and pieces of the memories I can remember."

"We don't have to discuss the details. We can just discuss your feelings." He grabs his pen and paper again and scribbles down some notes. "I think that's something we'll work on in your next session. In the meantime, I'm going to teach you some relaxation exercises to help calm yourself down when you're having a panic attack."

"I wish it were that easy, because I want her to be able to touch me, but I just don't see it working." I nervously crack my knuckles. "I always panic whenever things get too far."

"It'll take some time, but I have all the confidence that you'll eventually get to a place in your life where you'll be able to handle physical contact. Do you want to know why?" he asks, and I nod. "Because you want to get better. I can tell. And wanting to overcome something is the first step to getting there."

I hope he's right. God, do I hope. But until I see proof,

I won't be able to believe it.

"What about my memories? I don't want to stop doing the therapy." Don't want to give up on Sadie.

"We're not stopping," he promises. "We're just taking a short break and giving your mind some time to settle."

I curl my fingers in and stab my nails into my palm as guilt crashes through me.

Sadie, I'm so sorry.

Sorry, sorry, sorry.

Sorry I can't find you,

Sorry I've forgotten,

Sorry you have to suffer.

If I could, I'd take your place.

God, how I wish it were me instead of her.

What I wouldn't give to make that happen.

Chapter 6

Lyric

“I love the smell of spring,” I declare as I inhale the delicious scent of the air. “It always makes me smile.”

“Everything makes you smile.” Ayden hands me a rag with a hint of a grin on his face.

It’s been a week since he sleepwalked, and for the most part, he seems to be okay. I’d put money on it, though, that he still feels guilty about the ordeal. Guilty because he worried everyone. Guilty because he freaked me out. My dear, shy boy, always worrying about everyone except himself. I wish I could talk to him about it without upsetting him, but after seeing him cry, I worry mentioning anything will trigger a nerve.

His parents—who I call Uncle Ethan and Aunt Lila, even though we’re not related—must have had the same thought process as me, because they seem pretty hush, hush about what happened.

“That’s not true.” I collect the rag from him and duck my head under the hood of my 1970 Dodge Challenger. My dad and I have been working on fixing it up since December, and I’m hoping to have it drivable soon. “Bugs don’t make me smile. Or frowny faces.”

He snorts a laugh. “Frowny faces? Only you would say frowns don’t make you smile.”

“That’s because I’m that awesome.” I pull the dipstick out and wipe it off with the rag before dipping it back inside the oil.

“That, you are,” he remarks, moving up behind me.

“And don’t ever forget that, my friend.” I remove the dipstick, glance at the oil level, then put the stick back in. Wiping my hand off with a rag, I step back from the car. “It looks like it might—” My back bumps into Ayden.

He hardly ever instigates contact first, expect on rare, amazing, wonder-filled occasions, so I allow myself to enjoy the earth-shattering moment and breathe in the feel of his body heat.

I smile stupidly when he doesn’t move away. “Whatcha doing?”

"Nothing." His voice is uneven, revealing his nerves. "I was just . . ." He releases a breath then places his hands on my hips. Surprisingly, his fingers are steady. "I just wanted to touch you." He rests his forehead against the back of my head and inhales deeply. "And to make sure you're okay."

"Okay about what?" My eyelids drift shut as I lean into his touch.

His simple touches are better than light.
They awaken my body and bring it to life.
More. More. More, my body is craving.
The addiction is potent, consuming, aching.
Leaves my body wanting, pleading, shaking.
Sometimes I feel like I'm withering, fading.
Fading. Fading. Fading.
Into him.

"About . . . about what happened the other day . . . when I sleepwalked." His fingers grasp onto me, and his chest crashes against my back as his shallow breaths turn ragged. "I know I probably freaked you out. I've been meaning to ask you about it, but I didn't want to upset you, so I decided to wait until stuff cooled off."

"I'm not upset about what happened." And not surprised one little bit that my theory about him was right. I turn around and loop my arms around him. "I'm just worried about you and how you're handling it."

"I'm fine," he swears, searching my eyes for my true feelings. He forgets, though, that I'm like an open book. "It's not anything I haven't dealt with before. But you . . . What did I say to you exactly while I was asleep?"

"Nothing I could really understand."

"Are you sure? Because, if I said anything weird . . . Then I want to know."

"The whole situation is a little strange," I admit. "You were completely out of it, yet you were standing there, talking and . . . crying."

"I cried?" His mouth curves to a frown. "I'm so sorry. I can't believe I did that in front of you."

"Stop worrying." I lure him closer to me with a jerk, the movement rougher than I intended. "You have nothing to be sorry about. You sleepwalk. So what? We all have our weird, little quirks."

He cracks a small, adorable smile. "And what are your weird, little quirks?"

"Um, hello, isn't that kind of obvious? I'm *always* as

freaking cheery and sparkly as the sun is on crack, trying to spin everything and everyone into sugar and rainbows with my smile. Albeit, it's an adorable smile." I flash him my pearly whites. "I bet it's kind of blinding and gets a little tiring to deal with all the time, though."

"It'll never get tiring." His mood shifts as his gaze drops to my lips. "And your smile's beautiful."

I have to take a moment to catch my breath; otherwise, my voice will wobble like mad-crazy. "You can kiss me if you want."

"Can I?" He tries to tease, but his voice comes out raspy.

Leaning in, he places his lips against mine, giving me a featherlike kiss.

"That's it?" I jut out my lip when he pulls away.

Sucking in a few calculated breaths, his hands glide around my back, and he fumbles with the hem of my tank top. "It's getting late, and your parents will be coming home soon. I don't want them to find us making out in the garage." When I crinkle my nose, he adds, "Lila and Ethan aren't going to be home for a while, though, so . . ."

"So, what?" I play dumb and totally get rewarded when he blushes.

"I thought we could, you know . . ." He lifts one hand to nervously massage the back of his neck. "Go up to my room for a while, and"—his blush deepens—"continue kissing."

I choke on a giggle. "I knew what you meant from the beginning, but it was fun watching you get all weirded out."

He jokingly scowls at me. "That was kind of mean."

"Yeah, I know. It's a good thing you love me." I instantly want to kick myself for dropping the L-bomb. I know the word makes him squeamish.

He stares at me, his expression unreadable, as silences encompasses us.

"So, yeah, let's go inside," I say awkwardly after a soundless moment goes by.

Not saying anything, he laces our fingers together and steers me out of the garage, down my driveway, and toward his house. He pauses when we're about to walk inside and suddenly looks down at the end of the driveway.

I track his gaze to Miss Finkleson, our neighbor across the street, watering her garden in her bathrobe. "What are you looking at?"

"Making sure my . . . babysitter isn't around." He tensely massages his neck.

"Babysitter? Dude, what are you talking about?" I squint at his expression. "Did you get high with Sage today?"

"No." He sighs, his hand falling to his side. "Because of everything going on, an undercover detective has been following me to make sure I'm safe. I didn't know it, though, and got caught going somewhere. Lila made it seem like, because I fucked up, I was going to be watched all the time, but I haven't noticed the car around for the last couple of hours."

"What were you doing?" I wonder. "When you got caught?"

He pulls an oh-I'm-so-busted expression. "Hanging out in front of that house Sadie last lived at. Figures the day I decide to go inside is the day they followed me. Lila was really fucking pissed off at me."

He went into that house?

A detective is following him?

To keep him safe?

I bite down on my lip hard as reality crushes down on me and causes my eyes to water up.

"Lyric, what's wrong?" He lowers his face closer to mine, searching my eyes. "Are you . . . ? Are you *crying*?"

"No," I lie, sucking back the waterworks. "I'm almost crying."

"Almost crying?" He frowns. "What'd I say that upset you?"

"It's not what you said. It's what you didn't say, which I know is a really cliché girlfriend thing to whine about." I blink up at the sunlight filtering through the sky, only because I can't look him in the eye at the moment. "I hate that you keep stuff from me. You going to that house is like the Internet hacker all over again."

"No, it's not." He cups my face between his hands, forcing me to look at him. "I didn't tell you about this, because I was still trying to figure out for myself why the hell I felt the need to go there all the time." He smooths his hands down my cheeks, down my neck and shoulders, leaving a trail of heat all the way to my waist. "I realized I was searching for something I'd never really find, so I won't be going back."

"Good. You should have never gone there by yourself, ever. Not with all this stuff going on. It's too dangerous."

"I couldn't go back even if I wanted to. Not when that detective is keeping an eye on me." He contemplates something. "It was weird, though. While I was there, a woman came up to me and told me it wasn't safe for me to be there. But it was raining, and she had the hood of her coat pulled up so I couldn't see her face."

"That's strange," I agree, trying not to go all crazy-girlfriend on him. But he has me incredibly worried that he's going to do something stupid. "Did you tell Lila about her?"

"Yeah, she called Detective Rannali, and he said he'd look into it, but I guess the area where the house is has a high crime rate, especially with drugs, and he seems pretty convinced the woman was just warning me to get the hell out of the area."

I step closer, eliminating the space between us. "Ayden, promise me, the next time you're going to try something questionable, you'll tell me first. I know you have this whole belief that you need to do everything alone so you won't burden everyone with your problems, but I want to be burdened. No, I *need* to be burdened."

He presses his lips together and nods once. "All right. I promise."

"Thank you." I free a breath of relief. "I always need to know you're okay." I step back and twine my fingers with his. "Now, let's go inside and make out."

His lips threaten to pull upward as he turns and leads me the rest of the way to the back door. I can feel the beat of his heart pulsating from his fingertips as we enter his house.

It's quiet inside, soundless inside.

"So, no one's home at all?" I ask as we kick off our shoes in the foyer.

He shakes his head, giving me a nervous, sidelong glance. "Nope, everyone's gone for at least another hour."

Biting back a smile, I let him steer me into the kitchen. The air smells like cinnamon and chocolate, and I spot a plate of cookies on the counter.

"Yes! Cookies!" I exclaim a little too excitedly. Aunt Lila owns her own catering business and is an amazing cook. "I love it when she bakes."

He laughs at me as I swipe a cookie from off the plate. Then we start up the stairway.

As we reach the top of the stairs, he smiles at me from over his shoulder as I stuff my face with gooey chocolate.

"Good?"

"Delish." I lick my fingers clean, making exaggerated smacking sounds.

He watches me in complete fascination, his eyes burning with something I don't quite recognize.

I lick my last finger clean. "Are you okay?"

He blinks and then clears his throat. "Yeah, I'm good."

I eye him suspiciously. "Wait. Are we having another office moment?" I restrain a laugh when he uncomfortably shifts his weight, a flush creeping up his cheeks.

Back in the day, before we were dating, he got a hard-on while I was straddling his lap. Being slightly intoxicated, I pointed it out and embarrassed the crap out of him.

"Honestly," he starts, carefully calculating his next words, "we've had a lot of office moments over the last few months."

Acting like a ridiculously silly girl, I grin. "Really?"

"I don't know why you look so shocked," he quickly says, looking off over my shoulder. "Just looking at you is—does—turns me on. But kissing and touching you . . ." He blinks back at me. "But, yeah, anyway . . ." He waits, looking hopeful that I'll let him off the hook.

Even though I love teasing him, I decide to go easy on

him. "So, anything else interesting happening in your life that I should know about?"

He contemplates it, climbing to the top of the stairs. "Well, I'm getting my tattoo covered in a few days."

"Really?" I ask excitedly.

He nods, excited himself. "I'm a little nervous about . . . well"—he gestures at his side where the tattoo is hidden beneath his shirt—"the whole process."

I offer him an encouraging smile. "You'll do fine. I know it. And, if you want, I can go with you and hold your hand."

"Actually, I was kind of hoping you'd sketch the cover up tattoo for me." He skims his finger along the inside of my wrist, causing me to shiver. "It'd be nice if you'd go with me, too, though."

"Of course." I puff out a stressed breath. "Man, I'm feeling a little bit nervous."

"About what?"

"About creating something that will permanently be on your body. Just think, every time you look at it, you'll think of me."

His brow arches questioningly. "And that's a bad

thing?"

I shrug. "That all depends on stuff."

"Stuff like what?"

"I don't know, like if we break up one day or something."

He studies me with his dark eyes, and my skin starts to heat; not with a blush, but with lust. My heart pumps fast, dances in my chest, creates a rhythm of its own, a beat that would make a fantastic song.

"I think I'm okay with something you draw being on my body forever." Without warning, his lips come down on mine hard, giving me barely any time to process more than a single thought about what he's said.

I have zero time to suck in a breath as his tongue slips into my mouth. He kisses me fiercely, passion burning, scorching through my body, silk spilling through my veins. It's the kind of kiss with zero planning, the kind of kiss that means so much. The kind of kiss I'll hold onto forever. The kind of kiss everyone should experience at least once in their lifetime.

My hands find his shoulders, my fingertips delving into the fabric of his shirt as I try to keep my legs from giving out. As if he senses my inability to stay on my feet, his hands travel down my body, trembling the entire way, and he grips onto my thighs. With a deep inhale, he holds onto me tightly and picks me up.

When his body begins to quiver, I start to lower my feet to the ground, but he constricts his grasp on me, holding me in place. He counts to five under his breath then presses me closer until so much heat is coursing through me I can barely breathe. So, so much heat. I feel like I'm drowning in heat, yet I want to sink farther, let the warmth take me down and hold me there forever.

"Where are we going?" I whisper against his lips as he starts to move somewhere.

Pressing me even closer to him, he slides a hand underneath my butt. "To my room." His voice is uneven, off-pitch, gravelly.

I link my feet behind his back as he stumbles blindly down the hallway and kicks open his bedroom door. I get lost in the kiss, the feel of his hands, the beat of his heart slamming through his chest and against mine. I get so lost I barely notice anything around me until we're falling onto the mattress.

His solid body lands on top of me, but his arms brace

the weight of his fall. He pulls back to look down at me, breathing heavily, and panic flashes in his eyes.

"Are you okay?" I ask, cupping his cheek. "We can slow down if we need to. We always can."

"I'm fine." He gasps for air, battling to calm down. Once he's settled, he stares at me with strands of his hair in his eyes. "I know we can always stop, but I . . . I think I want to keep going."

I sweep his hair out of his eyes and let my hand linger on his scruffy cheek. I'm not sure what he means. Keep going? How far? More kissing? More touching? More . . . ?

My thoughts dissipate as his lips return to mine, and he gives me a deliberate, sensual, soul-stealing kiss. His hand wanders up the bottom of my skirt, slowly, slowly, slowly. Every brush of his fingers, every caress of his tongue is deliberate, which makes every second that much more erotic. His fingers stop moving the moment they reach the hem of my panties. He never takes it farther than this, and I haven't asked him to, even though I want to. Badly.

I gasp and wiggle below him, desperate for him to touch me more. For me to be able to touch him. Touch, touch, touch him all over. I want to touch him like he touches me.

Knowing he'll more than likely stop me, I dare to slide my fingers down his back and fiddle with the hem of his shirt, stealing a touch. When he doesn't budge, I test him further, delving my fingers under the fabric and caressing his bare flesh. I hold my breath, waiting for him to panic, which makes the kiss instantly turn awkward because I eventually have to suck in a huge breath.

"One . . . two . . . three," he whispers under his breath then kisses me deeper, kisses me through the awkwardness and back into the intensity of the moment.

I'm not sure what's up with the counting, and I don't really care. He's letting me touch him more than I ever have. I grasp onto the moment, inching my hands up his back and tracing a soft path up his spine. He either shakes or shivers from my touch—maybe a little bit of both.

"I can stop," I tell him when his breathing shifts to erratic.

He takes a few measured breaths. "No . . . You're okay. I can do this."

I sketch a line up and down his back. "So, are you . . . ? I mean, you can touch me." I actually blush. Yeah, I, Lyric Scott, blush. It's something I thought would never happen, and it feels so freaking weird.

Thankfully, Ayden's face is too close to mine to notice.

He nods, either to himself or to me, before he slips a finger into my panties. Nerves bubble in my stomach, about to burst. I try to prepare myself, but the instant he slides a finger inside me, I'm lost.

Gone. Gone. Gone.

Lost inside you.

Lost inside me.

Lost inside us.

I feel so alive.

Breathing, heart beating,

Needing, needing, needing.

I can hardly breathe,

Can hardly think

Past the pleading, pleading, pleading.

By the time I return to reality, I'm out of breath, and my pulse is soaring. Ayden is staring down at me with so much desire blazing in his eyes I barely recognize him.

"Was that okay? I mean, you don't regret it, right?" He smooths strands of my blonde hair out of my eyes.

"No regrets at all," I assure him breathlessly, fighting

back a grin, but eventually, a smile plasters across my face.

His fingers splay across my cheek and he traces a line below my eye. "You're so beautiful. I just . . ." He sighs and rolls off me.

"What are you doing?" I pout, rotating on my side.

He stares up at the ceiling with his arm draped across his forehead. "I just worry about you all the time. I mean, you're so happy and outgoing, and I worry I'm going to ruin it."

"You don't ruin anything, and you need to stop saying that."

"Not even when you can't touch me?"

I roll over to him and swing my leg across him, pushing myself up and straddling him. "I can't touch you, huh?"

His hands mold to my waist as he grasps on to me. "You know what I mean. We can't even take our relationship further." His cheeks redden as he looks away.

"We can't?" I challenge, reaching for the bottom of my shirt. I lift it up and tug it over my head, shaking out my hair. "I think we take it further every day."

His breathing speeds up as his grey eyes drink me in. "I've been working on some stuff to help calm me down when I'm panicking," he whispers. "I want to get better for you."

"Is that what the counting is about?"

He nods. "My therapist taught me some breathing exercises and stuff."

"While I love that you're trying, I still need you to know that it doesn't matter to me. I want to be with you, no matter what."

He leans up and kisses me, his hand sliding around my back. I shiver from the graze of his fingers against my flesh as he fumbles with the clasp of my bra. Once he gets it unfastened, the straps fall from my shoulders, and the cool air nips at my skin. Even though I'm pretending to be as cool as a freaking cucumber, my heart slams against my chest.

"Tell me if I need to slow down," he whispers against my lips.

Instead of telling him to go further, I grab his hands and place them on me. He groans from the touch, seeming in pain. But he has to be enjoying this since I can feel his happiness pressing between my thighs.

"Your skin's so soft," he murmurs, caressing the sensitive spot of flesh to the side of my breast.

I softly sketch his jawline with my fingertip. "So's

yours. And, one day when you're ready, I'll be able to touch you like you touch me."

His hands continue to explore my body, his fingers scorching hot against my flesh. "What if I'm never ready?"

"You will be, Ayden. You've come a long way already."

He sucks in a breath through his nose then pushes up and slams his lips to mine while his hand glides to my breast, his thumb grazing my nipple.

"You taste like cookies," he breathes softly through kisses.

"You taste like . . ." I trail off at the sound of a startled gasp from behind us.

"Oh, shit." I scramble off Ayden, grab my shirt, and press it to my chest.

"I'm sorry," Lila says from the doorway with her hand over her eyes. "I should have knocked first."

"No, you shouldn't have," Ayden sputters, bolting upright in the bed. "I mean, you shouldn't have had to, because we shouldn't have been in here, doing this . . . doing stuff." He rakes his fingers through his hair. "I'm so sorry."

Lila remains quiet with her hands over her eyes. “Okay, here’s what we’re going to do. I’m going to give you guys exactly one minute to get dressed and meet me downstairs. Then we’re going to have a talk. And, Lyric, I’m calling your parents and having them come over, as well.”

I pull a face. Great. This is going to be so awkward. “Okay.”

“Good.” She hurries away, leaving the door wide open.

I quickly put my bra on then yank my shirt over my head. “Well, looks like the cat’s out of the bag now,” I say as I hop off the bed.

“This is so bad.” Ayden stands up, wrapping his arms around his head, freaking out.

“Yeah, but we were going to tell them eventually.” I adjust my shirt into place.

He paces the floor in front of his bed. “But not like this . . . not after she saw me. And I need to prepare myself for how disappointed your parents are going to be.”

“Disappointed?” Confused, I step in front of him, forcing him to stop moving. “Why would they be disappointed? A little angry, sure, but they’ll get over it.”

He gulps. “Not over what happened. With me. I doubt

they're going to be happy that you're with me."

I gape at him. "Are you kidding me right now?"

"I know who I am." He refuses to look at me, staring at a poster on the wall. "I have so many problems . . . My life is so fucked up. You're so perfect, and they're not going to want me ruining that for you."

"First of all, I'm not perfect, and my parents definitely don't think I am. There've been many lectures and punishments proving how imperfect I am, just like everyone else in the world. And, second of all, I honestly think they've been expecting this to happen between us."

He shakes his head, his jaw set tight. "I highly doubt that."

I roll my eyes. "You're being ridiculous right now, and I'm going to prove it."

I grab his hand and march for the door, ready to face the music. Ready to prove him wrong.

He is good for me.

Everyone knows it.

Everyone knows just as much as I do that we're meant to be together.

Chapter 7

Ayden

I'm a nervous wreck going downstairs. Even though I knew our relationship would eventually be discovered, I expected it to happen later on and definitely not under such embarrassing circumstances. Now, they're really going to start keeping an eye on me.

"Dude, breathe," Lyric mutters under her breath as we reach the bottom of the stairway. "Everything's going to be fine."

I wish that were true. Tonight was so amazing—touching her like that, watching her fall apart beneath me. She tastes and feels so good that, if I had my way, I'd spend every hour of my life feeling her skin and kissing her.

Life would be so much easier if that were possible, but that's hardly plausible. The reality of the situation is ugly and brutal and is about to become a whole lot more so.

My heart is hammering in my chest as we walk into the living room. Our hands are linked together, but the moment I catch sight of Ethan and Lila, I wrench mine away.

Lyric sighs at my movement then plops down on the sofa, appearing completely comfortable.

"So, what's the punishment?" she asks, crossing her legs and relaxing back in the sofa.

"That's for your parents to decide," Lila replies with aggravation written all over her face. "But I'm just going to say that you are way too comfortable about the situation, young lady."

"I'm not too comfortable. Not really," Lyric protests. "I just know that this shouldn't be as big of a deal as you guys are going to make it. I mean, from the stories I've heard you guys and my parents tell each other when you guys drink too much wine, you all had sex by the time you were our age."

Lila's lips part in shock. "You're having sex?"

"No, we're not," I interrupt, my voice higher than normal. "We were just . . ." I trail off, my cheeks warming with my mortification.

Ethan offers me a sympathetic look, seeming about as uneasy as I am.

"Whether we are or aren't having sex is beside the point." Lyric shoots me a dirty look from over her shoulder. "The point is that we're legally adults, and if we were having sex, it wouldn't be the end of the world."

I press her with a stressing look. *You're making this worse,* I mouth.

She carries my gaze with determination, but then sighs. "Fine, I'll let us get our lecture. I was just trying to prove a point."

Lila and Ethan sit with their mouths hanging open, at a loss for words. The room goes so silent everyone can probably hear the thunderous beat of my heart.

After a minute passes, I sink down on the opposite side of the sofa from Lyric. When the front door swings open, though, I spring up from the sofa and decide to sit on the chair across the room, way, way far away from Lyric.

"So, what'd they do now?" Mr. Scott asks, rubbing his hands together as he enters the room.

Beside him, Mrs. Scott doesn't look as relaxed. I almost wonder if she already knows what's going on.

"I . . ." Lila starts, but stops herself. "Well, I guess

there's no easy way to put it other than I caught them, um, messing around in the bedroom."

Mr. Scott's expression instantly plummets. "You caught them doing *what*?"

I slouch lower in the chair with my head ducked and fix my attention on the floor.

"It wasn't that big of a deal," Lyric intervenes. "It's not like we were having sex or anything."

"Not that big of a deal." Mr. Scott seems irritated, which kind of surprises me.

Out of the two of them, he has always been more laid back than Lyric's mother.

"Oh, don't seem so shocked," Mrs. Scott says, sounding calmer than all of them. "She's eighteen, and her best friend's a guy she spends every waking hour with. Sounds a little bit familiar, doesn't it?"

"You were nineteen," Mr. Scott argues. "And that was different. We were both more mature than her."

"Hey," Lyric argues, offended, "I'm mature."

"Yeah, okay. We were so mature," Mrs. Scott talks over Lyric, her voice dripping with sarcasm. "We never did anything reckless at all."

"Well, okay, I get your point, but still . . . You and I aren't like our parents," Mr. Scott replies defensively. "We have rules. We need to put those rules into play and ground her or something."

I still haven't looked up, my eyes trained on the floor as I wait for one of them to say something negative about Lyric being with me. But they continue on about their pasts as if they've forgotten about the problem and the other people in the room, listening to their every word.

Finally, they must remember that other people are around, because Mrs. Scott hisses, "Maybe we should talk to Lyric about this at home."

"Sounds good to me," Mr. Scott agrees, clearly annoyed.

I don't look up even though I feel Lyric's eyes on me.

"They're gone. You can look up now," Ethan says after the front door clicks shut.

I elevate my gaze to find that Ethan and Lila are watching me with concern. Their change in demeanor throws me for an unexpected turn.

I wait for them to say something, punish me, tell me how badly I messed up. Instead, they remain silent for a mind racing amount of time before they exchange a look, and then Ethan gets to his feet.

"You want to go out to the garage and help me change the oil in the truck?" Ethan asks me, although it's not really a question.

Nodding, I stand up and follow him through the house and out the back door. It's past seven o'clock at night, and usually, the family is sitting around the table, eating dinner. I'm guessing tonight we might be breaking the routine, though.

Ethan doesn't say much as we start working on the oil. I hand him tools whenever he asks for them and help him when he needs it. So much time ticks by that I don't think he's going to bring up what happened. When he finishes, he cleans the oil off his hands, and then an uneasy look crosses his face.

My lecture and punishment are coming, and I tell myself I can handle it, that I've been through way worse.

"So, you and Lyric, huh?" He tosses the rag aside on the shelf and shuts the hood of the truck. "Can't say I'm that surprised."

"I'm sorry I messed up," I tell him because I don't know what else to say. The fact that he doesn't think it's surprising is baffling to me.

He reclines against the front of the truck with his arms folded. “You didn’t really mess up. I was young once, too. I get it.”

I rest against the shelf behind me. “I’m not sure Mr. Scott would agree with you. He seemed pissed. I’m afraid he’s not going to let me spend any more time with her.”

He waves me off. “He’ll get over it. He just needs some time to cool off.”

“If it helps, I promise nothing like that will happen again.”

“Don’t make promises you can’t keep.” He heads for the door. “Just make sure that you’re careful with stuff, okay?”

Is this some sort of subtle safe sex talk? Why isn’t everyone freaking out more?

“Okay,” I reply uneasily as we leave the garage.

When we reach the porch, he stops to pat me on the shoulder. “You’re a good kid, even if you don’t always think so.”

I feel lost. It somehow feels like he knows my fear of unworthiness. “Thanks.” I start to wonder if maybe Dr. Gardingdale was right. Maybe my unworthiness is in my head, my own inner demon that no one else can see. I only wish I could find a way to get completely past it.

Wish on a thousand stars that, one day, somehow, my life will be normal.

Chapter 8

Ayden

Dinner is pretty normal. The only exception is Fiona teasing me about Lyric, but I can handle that. Thankfully, Kale has moved on from his crush on Lyric, so I don't have to worry about him getting upset.

"I can't believe you guys fooled around with the door open," Fiona teases with a smirk as she butters a roll.

"Fiona Gregory," Lila warns as she passes the bowl of corn to Everson, "leave your brother alone."

Fiona dramatically rolls her eyes but does as she's told, keeping her lips zipped.

"Now, let's talk about something else," Lila says cheerfully. "Does anyone have anything exciting happening in their life?"

"I finally asked Mandy out," Kale says, cutting into his steak. "We're going to a movie on Friday, if that's okay?"

"Who's Mandy?" Ethan asks, pouring himself some wine. "I thought you had a thing for Lyric." He pulls a whoops face. "Sorry, I probably shouldn't go there, right?"

"I stopped liking Lyric when I found out Ayden was dating her." Kale reaches across the table for the butter.

Lila stares at Kale in shock. "Wait? How long have you known about them?"

Kale gives a noncommittal shrug. "I don't know. For, like, a couple of months."

Lila's eyes narrow on me. "You two have been together for *months*?"

"Um . . ." I rub the back of my neck. "Kind of."

"I figured as much when I saw you guys backstage at the concert," Ethan absent-mindedly remarks as he drenches his steak in barbeque sauce.

"And what happened backstage?" Lila seems to grow angrier by the second.

Ethan sets down the bottle of sauce then picks up his fork and knife. "I thought I caught them when they were about to kiss."

"Why didn't you say anything until now?" she asks, sounding hurt.

"Yeah, I'm sorry about that, but I knew, if it was true, everyone would act all crazy, which you guys did." He starts slicing his steak. "I figured I'd let them tell you when they were ready and give them some time without constantly being pressured."

Lila's shoulders slump in defeat. "All right, you have a point." She frowns as if greatly disappointed by that fact. "You're off the hook."

"Thanks," Ethan says, shooting me a discreet smile.

I chuckle under my breath and reach for the bowl of potatoes.

"So, I want to go to football camp this summer," Everson announces, breaking the silence.

I'm extremely grateful as the conversation shifts from me to him. I remain fairly quiet for the rest of dinner, lost in my thoughts about what happened in my bedroom with Lyric. How she traced her fingers up and down my back. How I was terrified out of my mind, afraid of the memories clipping at the surface. Afraid because . . . It felt too fucking nice. I found myself wanting to explore more, and that scared me out of my goddamn mind.

I've never felt like that before.

You make me feel things I didn't know were

real.

How can that be possible?

I thought I was never going to be whole again,

That I'd remain a broken shell,

Cracked in places that could never be fixed.

Now, everything I believed is withering,

Fading into something I can't explain.

Please, please, don't let me down.

Give me hope

And let me fade away.

"Ayden, are you all right?" Lila interrupts my thoughts.

I rip myself from my daze, realizing I'm the only one left at the table.

"Yeah. Sorry. I guess I just zoned off." The legs of the chair scrape against the tile floor as I scoot back from the table.

"Okay." She picks up an empty bowl and carries it to the sink. "Would you mind helping me do the dishes? There's something I'd like to talk to you about."

I start stacking the dirty plates on the table. "What's

up?"

"Well, I talked to Detective Rannali about letting you read the letter your sister wrote, like you asked." She opens the dishwasher and places a few plates inside. "Unfortunately, they can't let you read the letter yet, because it's important evidence as of now."

Even though I was expecting that answer, it's still frustrating.

"Okay, thanks for trying." My shoulders sink as reality crushes me down into the ground.

Down. Down. Down.
Into the dirt,
Burying me alive, right along with the hurt.
Suffocating, smothering, where is the air?
Hidden with the pain in a sea of despair.
Down. Down. Down,
Into the dirt.
Pull me from the despair, help me survive.
Please, someone help me.
Don't let me die.
Lift me from the darkness and into the light—
Out of the dirt, out of the pain, away from

the hurt.

She abruptly folds her arms around me. "I know life's been hard on you, and while I really don't ever want to walk in on you like that again, I'm glad you're with Lyric. You deserve the best, Ayden, and I know Lyric makes you happy, which is why I'm not going to punish you over what I walked in on tonight." She clears her throat. "Just promise me you two will be careful."

This is quickly turning into the most mortifying conversation I've ever had.

"Okay, but . . . never mind."

She moves back to look at me. "No, go ahead and say it. I need to know that you feel comfortable enough with me."

"It really isn't that big of a deal." I wave it off. "Forget I said anything."

"Is it about Lyric or . . . sex?"

"What? No. It's definitely not that." I make myself look her in the eye. "It's about Sadie and the case. I just want to know more about what's going on."

She stiffens. "Look, Ayden, I know you're worried about her, but the police are doing everything they can to find her. They even tracked down that woman you ran into in that godawful neighborhood and brought her in for questioning."

"What'd they find out?"

"Nothing much." She grabs another plate out of the sink and sticks it in the dishwasher. "The woman said she saw you go into the house, and she thought she'd warn you to stay away from it, considering what happened there. They already knew what went on there, though, so her statement didn't help with the case."

I gather a few dirty cups out of the sink and hand them to her. "But I want to know exactly what happened in that house. No one's flat out told me the details."

She remains quiet while she stacks the cups on the dishwasher rack. "The police believe Sadie was taken from that house by the group of people who took you guys when you were younger, and the foster parents she was living with at the time of the kidnapping were drug addicts and didn't notice she was missing for over a week, so it instantly put a hitch in the case."

A week? She was gone and entire week, and no one knew?

My heart is splitting in two

And bleeding out

Because she never knew

Just how good life could be.

I grip on to the edge of the counter to keep from falling down. "Didn't they notice all the paint and stuff on the walls?"

"They might have, but . . ." She sighs heavily. "When people are on drugs, they can get too caught up in their addiction."

"My mother was an addict," I utter quietly with my head lowered. "She was like that sometimes, so I get it. But still, it pisses me off."

"I know it does, sweetie." When I glance up, her heart looks like it's breaking for me. "What can I do to make you feel better?"

"The only way I think I'll ever feel better again is when they find her." Forcing myself to suck it up, I stand up straight. "There's some stuff on the Internet about the locations of some of the places the Soulless Mileas hang out at, and I think you should mention them to the detective the next time you talk to him."

Her brows knit. "I didn't know you were looking up

that sort of stuff on the Internet."

"No one really tells me anything, so I thought I'd find out some stuff for myself." I hand her a dish soap tablet from the box beside the sink, and she drops it inside the dishwasher.

"We tell you what we feel is a healthy amount." She closes the dishwasher door and pushes start. "Does your therapist know you've been doing this?"

"No. The only person I've told is Lyric and now you. I didn't think it was that important."

"I think you should tell him so you two can talk about the stuff you've read. It can't be easy . . . reading about that . . ." The way she says it makes me wonder if she has been reading stuff, too. She grabs a dishtowel and begins wiping down the counters. "Maybe I'll mention it to him myself since I have to go in for a visit, anyway."

A pucker forms between my brows. "Why are you going in for a visit?"

She winds around the kitchen island, cleaning up spilled sauce on the tile. "To discuss your amnesia therapy." She stops scrubbing and looks up at me. "Your father and I just feel like maybe you should stop doing it since there hasn't been a lot of progress, and it seems to be increasing your stress."

"It's not increasing my stress." The last thing I ever want to do is stop with the therapy, and if Lila gets involved, there's a slim chance I'll ever be allowed to do it again. "And I can't do that to my sister—stop trying like that."

"You've been sleepwalking more ever since you started the treatment. You sleep less. And now I find out you're looking up stuff on the Internet. It's not healthy."

"Nothing about any of this will ever be healthy, but I might be able to be less stressed if the police find her." I contemplate my next words carefully. "Which is why I think you should reconsider letting me try that experimental therapy."

She swiftly shakes her head. "We've already talked about it and decided it was too risky."

I grit my teeth, biting back my anger. I don't agree with her, but at the same time, I feel guilty for even thinking about going against them. The Gregorys were kind enough to take me in when they knew I had so many problems, and I owe them for that. The last thing I need to do is yell at her.

"I'm going to go up to my room and work on my homework." I swing around her and stride for the stairway.

"Ayden, please don't be angry with me," she calls out. "We're doing this because . . . because we love you."

I smash my lips together so forcefully my jaw aches. Despite the fact that I once had a mother and father, I've never actually had anyone say they love me like that. I don't even know how to respond, so I don't say anything, hurrying up the stairs and locking myself in my room.

Lock yourself up.

When are you ever going to learn?

The only way to be free

Is to give in.

The only way to be free

Is to surrender.

Chapter 9

Ayden

About an hour into writing my English essay, I decide I need a break and get on my computer. I open up the webpage I've looked at every night for the last couple of weeks that contains an article about the Soulless Mileas and their rituals and beliefs. On the top of the page are photos of houses, backyards, the shore—the pictures I mentioned to Lila.

I shut my eyes and try to summon locked up memories.

The house on the hill
Bleeds through the ground,
Saturates the dirt,
And drips from the trees.
The red river flows down the grass
And to the ocean.
Waves crash against the sand,

Erasing the blood

And carrying it away.

But a faint trail still remains.

The house on the hill

Waits to be found,

Waits to tell its secrets

Of shackles and nails,

Stories of torture and pain.

Drip.

Drip.

Drip.

"What is that, Ayden?" my sister whispers through the darkness.

The only thing I can see is the bright pink ribbon in her hair.

I open my mouth to tell her, but my voice gets lost in the sound of the dripping.

"Ayden, can you hear me?" she whispers. "I think . . . I think it's blood. Oh, Ayden, I think it's my blood."

My eyes snap open as my body trembles from the memory—my sister's plea for help. I glance at the computer screen and examine the photos closely.

"Where are you, Sadie?" I whisper, my eyes locking

on a photo of a house settled on a shallow hill.

I try to picture the people inside it, but my memory shuts down. The strange thing that doesn't make sense to me is that the house we were trapped in was the one in my neighborhood and not on a hill. That's where I remember being dropped off by my mother, and that's where we were picked up, yet sometimes, I see us in other places and wonder if we were moved around somehow.

Overwhelmed with emotion, I leave the computer desk and seek comfort in my guitar. After I get situated on my bed, I pluck the strings with my fingertips and sing aloud, something I only do behind closed doors.

"Burning, burning, burning,
My body is in flames.
The fire igniting,
Burning me with rage.
I want the fire out,
Beg the clouds to drench me in rain.
Yet, when I look up,
The sky is fucking tame, no rain in sight.
So the fire keeps on burning,
Blazing, blazing, blazing,

Until it kills me eternally."

I frown at my words. With everything going on, I need to pick myself up, not drag myself further down into depression.

What I need is Lyric.

Glancing out my widow, I look over at her house. Her bedroom light is off, which means she's probably downstairs with her parents. I'm curious what her punishment is, but too nervous to text her and ask. Worried she'll tell me her parents won't let her see me again.

Sighing, I reach for my journal and turn to a page I've been scribbling in for the last week or so. I place my guitar on my lap again, line my fingers with the strings, and open my mouth.

"Lyric, Lyric, Lyric,
Her name pours through my veins.
Her laughter, her smile,
It's enough to drive me insane.
The way she looks at me,
It doesn't make sense
Why she would want me.
I don't understand.
She's so beautiful, so wild, so full of light.

Every time we touch,

Everything feels right.

Every time we kiss,

My head spins out of control.

I try to hold on, but I eventually fall.

Falling, falling, falling,

I'm falling into her.

Falling so blindingly, so helpless, so willingly.

Please, God, please, let me keep falling."

I stop strumming the strings as my phone buzzes on the nightstand. I set the guitar aside and check the incoming message.

The second I see her name, I smile.

Lyric: So, I just had a super awkward safe sex talk that lasted over an hour. What about you? Did you get punished?

I rest against the headboard and type a response.

Me: Ethan kind of the did the same thing with me, only his lasted about fifteen seconds. That's the only punishment you got? Your dad seemed pissed off.

Lyric: He was freaking out, but honestly, it was

kind of funny. I think he's having issues with me growing up or something. My mom was pretty chillax, though. Which I was kind of surprised about. I mean, she's usually the one doing all the scolding and punishing, but she seemed more worried that we're being careful.

Me: You told them that wasn't an issue, right?"

Lyric: Whoops. I knew I was forgetting something.

Me: Please tell me you're kidding! Your dad's never going to let me see you again if he thinks that.

Lyric: You should know that I'm kidding. I like my jokes, but I'm not a liar. And FYI, my dad wasn't upset because he thought I was sleeping with you. He was upset about the concept of his daughter having sex. They both seemed super relieved that it was you I was caught with and put a lot of the blame on me. I think they think I'm a bad influence on you, which might be kind of true. They like you, dude, even if you did get caught feeling their daughter up.

Me: Still, we should probably be a little bit more careful from now on.

Lyric: I'm good with being careful, just as long as there's going to be a from now on. You seemed freaked

out, Shy Boy, and that stuff you said about my parents being disappointed that I was with you . . . It makes me sad that you see yourself like that, that you can't see how good you are.

Me: I'm sorry I freaked out. What can I do to make it up to you?

Lyric: Hmm . . . Let me think. How about admitting that you're good enough for me?

Me: I'm being serious. I want to make it up to you.

Lyric: And I'm being serious. I want you to say it.

When I don't respond right away, another text buzzes through.

Lyric: I'm being serious. Say it or else.

I can't help myself.

Me: Or else what?

Lyric: Ah, I think I'm being challenged.

A pause then another message comes through.

Lyric: If you don't tell me that you're good enough for me, I won't kiss you for a week.

I chuckle.

Me: Fine. I'm good enough for you. There, are you happy?

Lyric: I'm really happy, actually. Not only did I get you to say it, but now I know how much you love my kisses.

Me: You should have known that already.

Lyric: Maybe I did, but it's nice to know for sure. I have to go. My mom is making me watch a show with them. God knows what it's about. Probably a tutorial on how to accurately put a condom on or something.

I shake my head, grinning. Leave it to Lyric to get me to smile even when I've had the most depressing night.

When we say goodbye, I put my phone away and spend the next hour working on my homework. By the time I fall asleep, I think I'm feeling better until I sink into a nightmare of the woman with hair that matches her blood red fingernails.

Drip.

Drip.

Drip.

"Close your eyes and prepare yourself, Ayden." Fingernails slide across my hands, up my arms, and down my chest, making my gut twist with disgust. "I'm going to break you apart and make you bleed."

Chapter 10

Lyric

It's Friday night, which means concert time for my band, Alyric Bliss. Well, concert might be a stretch. Basically, we have a gig at Infinite Bliss, my father's club, opening for another band. We play five songs total, and my dad is making us sing our own stuff in order to prep us for when we record.

"You look nervous." Sage, the drummer of our band, remarks. With his blue hair, multiple piercings and tattoos, and edgy clothing, Sage looks the part. "I thought you'd be over your stage fright by now."

"I *am* over it." When I peer out at the packed room, my body contradicts my words as a thousand butterflies on crack start to flutter inside my stomach.

"You pointing it out isn't helping, so stop being a dick," Nolan, our bassist, tells Sage while twisting the knobs of the bass he's holding. Nolan is a little less grunge and more boy band-ish: spikey blond hair and blue eyes with these crazy full lips that don't seem like they should belong to a guy. But he plays a sick guitar solo, so he's cool in my book.

Sage tosses a drumstick in the air then catches it like a baseball. "I'm not being a dick. I'm just stating the obvious—that she looks nervous for it being our seventh performance." I scowl at Sage, and he raises his inked hands in front of him. "Sorry, I'll stop saying it."

"Thank you." I peer back at the floor, and my stomach drops again.

Even though I won't admit it aloud, Sage is right. It seems like I should be over my stage fright by now, yet before every performance, I feel as jittery as I do when I drink too much coffee.

"And where the hell is Ayden?" Sage says from behind me. "He should have been here by now."

"He'll be here," I assure him. Still feeling a little concerned myself, I decide to text him.

Me: We're on in like 40. You're on your way, right?

When he doesn't reply right away, I start to get all

twitchy. With the Soulless Mileas out there constantly tormenting him, it's hard to remain calm whenever he goes MIA.

After five minutes drag by, I squeeze through the mob of intoxicated people to get to the bathroom and check my appearance. I'm not really a makeup girl, but I reapply the kohl liner around my bright green eyes and dab on some lip gloss. Then I comb my fingers through my long, blonde hair, smooth my hands over my black shirt and plaid skirt, and tighten the laces on my red boots. The last thing I ever want to happen is tripping over my shoelaces.

After I'm done, I push out the door and head back to the stage. As I'm passing the bar, I notice a woman staring at me. She's very model-esque: long legs, flowing blonde hair, and bright blue eyes.

"Hey," she says, giving me a tentative wave.

"Um . . . hey." I have no clue who she is, but she acts like she knows me.

"You don't know who am I, do you?" she asks with a mixture of amusement and nervousness.

I shake my head. "Sorry."

"No worries." She rises from the barstool, scooping up

a half-filled wine glass from the counter. "I'm Ava. I used to know your mother and father back when they lived in Wyoming. I was out here visiting and heard your father had a club, so I thought I'd stop by."

The name doesn't ring a bell, but my parents rarely talk about the people they knew back in Wyoming.

"That's cool. You should track my dad down and say hi." I scan the bar then the hallway that leads to my dad's office. "He's around here somewhere, more than likely in his office, but he wanders out here during performances."

"Lyric!" Sage hollers from the backstage area with his hands cupped around his mouth. "Time to get your ass up here!"

I roll my eyes at him. "Sorry. I guess I have to go. But, seriously, go say hi to my father. I'm sure he'll want to chat with you about the good ol' days or whatever."

She offers me a small smile when I wave, and then I hurry through the crowd. My heavy boots clunk against the steps as I dash up the stairway to the backstage.

"Dude, Sage, my bro, my friend, what are you thinking, screaming across the stage like that?" I ask as I duck behind the curtain. "My dad's not going to be happy with you acting like a spastic mad man."

Sage gives me an innocent look. "I tried to text, but you didn't answer."

I check my phone and realize the battery is now dead. "Has Ayden texted you yet?"

Sage shakes his head. "And I've texted him like fifty times."

As I grow even more worried, I open my mouth to tell Sage to hand me his phone so I can call Lila and Ethan, but then the door to our right swings open.

Ayden rushes inside with his guitar case in hand. "Sorry, I'm late. My car was being a pain in the ass and wouldn't start." His hair is dripping wet, water beads his skin, and his soaked grey shirt clings to his body.

I gawk at him like a pervert.

If you want to see perfection,

Just look right in front of you.

So gorgeous and flawless

With dark, haunted eyes,

Lips that taste so intoxicating,

A body that . . .

Good God, that body.

I want touch it, run my hands all over him.

"Lyric, did you hear what I said?" Ayden interrupts my lustful thoughts.

I rip my eyes off his body. "Nope, not a damn word."

He inquisitively glances down at his shirt then back at me. "You okay?"

"Yep, I'm great. I was just"—I shrug—"checking your sexy body out."

Astonishingly, he doesn't blush as our gazes meld. It's been a week since we got caught in his bedroom, and we've been trying to behave ourselves, but behaving has increased the sexual tension to about an . . . oh, eleven hundred.

Sage clears his throat and shatters the moment into oblivion.

Even though he seems fine with Ayden and me being together, sometimes, when we show a little PDA, he gets annoyed.

"Why didn't you answer your texts?" Sage asks Ayden as he stuffs his drumsticks into the back pocket of his jeans.

Ayden blinks his attention away from me. "You texted me?" When Sage nods, he pats his pockets. "Shit, I must have left my phone at the therapist's office."

"You scared us," I tell Ayden. "Or at least me. I think Sage was more worried we wouldn't have a guitarist."

"Hey, I was kind of worried," Sage gripes. "I'm not that big of a douche."

"Fine, we were all worried." I lower my voice and lean in toward Ayden. "I thought something bad happened."

"It wasn't anything like that. Just car trouble, like I said. Everything's fine, though. The detective following me around helped me jumpstart it." He shakes his head, showering me with water.

"Gee, thanks for the shower," I tease, raising my hand to wipe the water off my face. "Is he still keeping an eye on you?"

"Yeah. Lila says it'll only be for a bit longer since nothing has happened in the last few weeks." He steps forward and gently brushes his fingers across my cheeks and lips. "I need you not to worry about me so much. I don't want you to panic every time I'm late." He places a featherlight kiss on my mouth. "I hate thinking that I stressed you out."

He tastes minty and smells like rain. I breathe in the scent and taste, softly sighing against his mouth like a lovesick girl.

"I can't stop worrying about you." My eyelashes flutter

as he tangles his fingers through my hair. “It’s part of the job title as your best friend.”

A soft groan slips from Ayden’s lips as his hands travel down my back.

Sage clears his throat again. “Get a room, would you? Jesus, it’s like one step away from watching porn.”

Ayden shakes his head at Sage. “So, what did I miss?” he asks me as he sets his guitar case on the floor.

“Well, we go on in, like, thirty,” I tell him then shoot Sage a conniving smile. “And Sage has been pissing his pants that you weren’t going to show up.”

Sage glares at me. “Yeah, right. You’re the one freaking out, and not just about Ayden.”

“What else are you freaking out about?” Ayden asks me with concern.

I give a shrug. “I already told you that I still get nervous every time we’re about to perform.”

“What can I do to help?”

“You could talk to me about something else. Take my mind off stuff.”

Nodding, he takes my hand and leads me back to the corner of the room. When he sits down on the floor, he pulls me down with him so we’re sitting across from each other.

"So, I've been talking to my therapist about that experimental therapy I told you about a while ago," he starts, resting against the wall.

"The one Lila doesn't want you to do?" I crisscross my legs and rest back on my hands.

He nods, fiddling with the leather bracelet I gave him. "But I'm not really sure she has any say in it anymore."

My head cocks to the side. "What do you mean?"

"I mean that I'm eighteen and technically don't need a guardian's permission to go through with the therapy." He leans forward and tugs on my arm, so I sit up straight. Then he laces his fingers through mine. "I don't want it to come to that," he says, staring down at our hands, "but, at the same time, I can't stop thinking about Sadie and how, if I could just see the people's faces, then maybe the police could track her down and make some arrests."

I take a minute or two to prepare myself for what I'm going to say next. "I get what you're saying—I really do—but what are the risks, exactly? I mean, how dangerous are we talking?"

"There's a short list of them," he answers with hesitancy. "Like memory loss and stress on the heart, but if the therapy's done right, then nothing should go wrong."

I make a mental note to search online for the side effects. If they're bad, then I'm going to talk him out of it. The last thing I ever want is for him to get hurt or, worse, lose him. My heart aches just thinking about it.

"Look, I get that, no matter what, it's kind of risky. And it's not going to be easy . . . seeing the stuff I've forgotten. I know my mind blocked it out for a reason." With his free hand, he scratches his head. "But I don't think I could live with myself if I didn't at least try. And I really need you to support me and be there for me."

Dammit. He said he needs me. There goes my plan of talking him out of it.

"All right, I can do that, I guess. But I'm not going to lie; I'm scared of what's going to happen. I don't . . ." I swallow hard. "I don't want to lose you." *Because I love you.*

> *I'm in love with you.*
> *Love you so much*
> *I feel like I'm going to combust,*
> *Shatter into pieces that scatter*
> *Through the wind and rain,*

Blow away and get lost.

Lost, lost, lost

In my love for you.

Now he's the one to gulp. "You won't. I promise."

"Hey, you two love birds, we're up!" Nolan shouts mockingly from behind us.

I crinkle my nose. "Sometimes, I wish you and I could just be a duo."

He smiles thoughtfully. "That'd be nice, but considering I can't sing, it'd be more of a solo and a half band."

"It still sounds better right now." I push to my feet and tug my skirt into place. "Those two are getting on my nerves."

He strokes my cheekbone with his finger. "Want me to throw a basketball at them to see if I can get them to shut up? I mean, I do still owe you for that."

Smiling, I ponder the idea. "While I know you're kidding, I'm seriously considering it."

"Well, let me know when you decide," he jokes, crouching down to unlatch his guitar case. "I'm going to go hurry and dry off the best I can before we go on."

"Why? You rock the wet shirt look pretty well."

He keeps his head tucked down. “Maybe, but I’d feel super awkward.”

“Well, you look sexy when you’re awkward, too.” I plant a kiss on the top of his head then squeeze through the curtains and skip off to set up with Sage and Nolan.

A few racing heartbeats later, Ayden joins us and hooks up his guitar to the amp while I adjust the microphone stand. The lights beam brightly and blind me to the point where I can hardly see anyone in the room. Still, I know they’re all out there, and those crazy ass butterflies in my stomach start taunting me again.

Thankfully, about a minute later, Sage slams the sticks against the drums, and Ayden strums the strings of his guitar. The sounds of the instruments block out my focus on the audience as my lips part.

“Rush. Rush. Rush.
My heart is rushing like the rain,
Erasing every ounce of pain from my body
And spilling it below me.
My sins bleed into the water,
Soaking through the ground.

Rush. Rush. Rush.

I close my eyes and feel myself disappear.

A skeleton of myself, a ghost of my soul,

I'll never give in to anyone.

I'll never go through this again.

Rush. Rush. Rush."

The lyrics are more morbid than what I normally sing, but I wrote them on a whim while I was bored one day and watched way too many depressing movies. When I sang it to my dad, he thought it rocked awesomeness, so I shared it with the band.

It's the first time I've sung it on stage before. The upbeat tempo has the crowd going wild, dancing and head banging, feeding me with the fuel I need to really get into the performance.

By the time I sang our full set, I'm dripping with sweat and grinning as I bounce backstage. Sage and Nolan high-five me on their way out, but Ayden seems a bit distracted. He passes by me without so much as a glance in my direction.

"What's up?" I chase after him, back past the curtain and to the flat area near the exit doors.

He carefully sets his guitar in the case. "It's nothing." His brows dip. "I just . . . I just had the strangest feeling someone was watching me, but I can't figure out why."

"Did you maybe see someone in the crowd that you know?"

"No, it's not that . . ." He trails off then shakes his head. "Never mind. I'm just being paranoid." When he faces me, he forces a smile. "Let's go celebrate your amazing performance."

"You sure?"

"Yeah, I'm sure. I want to celebrate my awesome performance, too." His lips quirk with genuine amusement.

I thrum my fingers together evil-villain style. "Hmmm, whatever shall we do?"

"Party." Sage appears out of nowhere like a freaking ninja with a bottle of champagne in his hand.

"Dude, did you jack that from the bar?" I reach for the bottle.

He dodges out of my reach. "Actually, I stole it from my mom's fridge. She has at least ten bottles of it, so she won't notice." He looks down at the bottle. "Although, I wish it were a bottle of Bacardi." He shrugs then grips the bottle in front of him and, with his thumb, pops the cork.

The bottle hisses and foam shoots all over the floor. I jump out of the path of the spraying foam while Sage takes a swig then offers me the bottle.

I take the drink from him. "I'm down, but you've totally got to take the fall for the mess on the floor if my dad finds out. I'm already on thin ice with him." I angle my head back and chug some champagne.

"Why? What'd you do?" Nolan asks, intrigued, as he joins our circle. He snatches the bottle from me after I lower it from my mouth and downs at least a quarter of the bottle.

I shrug, giving a discreet glance at Ayden. "Just some stuff."

"Stuff as in . . ." Sage's shifty gaze moves back and forth between Ayden and me questioningly. "Okay, never mind. Forget I asked." He pats his pockets. "I think I'm going to go outside and smoke." Which is code for him going outside, smoking, then hooking up with the first decent looking girl he can find.

He strides toward the exit door and pushes outside. Nolan throws back another swallow of champagne then shoves the bottle at me and hurries after Sage.

I take another sip then turn to Ayden. “You want some?” I ask, even though he more than likely will decline.

Neither of us are big drinkers, and Ayden doesn’t like doing it because he feels like he’s acting like his old self, the person he was before Aunt Lila and Uncle Ethan adopted him. So, I’m a bit startled when he grabs the bottle from me and takes a few swallows.

“You’re suddenly in a weird mood,” I remark as he hands the bottle back to me.

“I’m feeling pretty okay right now, maybe even good.” He laces his fingers through mine then stares at our interlocked hands with the faintest smile on his lips. From the sight of it, my insides get all gooey, like melted chocolate. “I was thinking we could hang out tonight and talk.”

Interesting, since he has never been a big talker.

“Okay, you want to go home, then, and hang out in one of our rooms? Or did you have something else in mind?”

“Remember the spot near the bridge that we used to hang out at back before we could drive?” he asks, and I excitedly bob my head up and down. “I was thinking we could go there.”

Goddamn those butterflies. They come to life the moment he says it. What the hell are they expecting to happen exactly?

“Yeah, we can do that.” I raise the bottle to my mouth and throw back a couple more sips. “I’ll go tell my dad we’re leaving and meet you at the car?”

Nodding, he collects his guitar case, and we part ways. I head down the metal stairs to the main floor, past the busy bar, and down the hallway right as the next band starts playing. Music flows through the building like warm honey and vibrates the floors.

“They have a good beat,” I comment aloud. “But we are definitely better.” I abandon the bottle of champagne before I reach the last door. “Hey, old man,” I tease as I enter my dad’s cluttered office. The walls are decorated with old music memorabilia, and the desk is covered with papers and wrappers. “I’m taking off. Just wanted to make sure you didn’t need anything.”

My dad glances up from some papers on his desk. He’s sporting his bedhead/fauxhawk, and he has a half empty beer next to him. “I actually needed to talk to you . . . Is the rest of your band still here?”

I shake my head and sink down in a chair across from his desk. “Nah, Nolan and Sage are doing God knows what, and Ayden's waiting for me out in the car."

My dad scrunches his nose. "You guys are going straight home, right?"

"We might make a stop or two on the way."

He frowns in disapproval. "I'd rather you go straight home."

"I won't be out late." I flash him a devious grin. "And don't worry, I put that condom Mom gave me in my pocket."

His skin pales. "Lyric, that isn't funny."

"It kind of is, though."

He rakes his fingers through his hair. "You're too much like me. It's driving me crazy."

"You used to think that trait was endearing." When he continues to veer toward a meltdown, I decide to let him off the hook. "Look, I wasn't lying the other night when I said I wasn't having sex yet, so would you please chill out? You're a cool dad and everything, but this whole awkward, freak-out thing you've been doing for the last week is making you lose mad cool points."

He rubs his hand down his face, leaving red marks on his skin. "I just don't want you to mess up your life by making a mistake."

"I won't. I promise." I draw an *X* across my heart. "Now, can you tell me what you wanted to talk to my band about, because it's been driving me crazy since you said it?"

"I said it a whole minute ago." He pauses, and I can tell he wants to bug me more about being careful but decides to drop it. "I think I might have an opportunity coming up for you guys."

I lean forward in the chair, eager to hear more. "What kind of an opportunity?"

His fingers wrap around his beer. "A tour kind of opportunity."

"Are you shitting me?" I bounce up and down with excitement.

"No, I'm not shitting you." He opens his drawer, pulls out a paper, and slides it across the desk to me. "It's this summer. It's not a huge tour or anything, and the bands are pretty unknown, but I think, for your first gig, this could be a really good thing."

"A really good thing." I snatch up the paper, jump from the chair, and run around the desk, throwing my arms around him. "This is the most awesomest thing ever."

He hugs me back. "Don't get too excited yet. You still have to see if everyone in your band can go, and we have to check with your mother and make sure it's okay. I know she's been talking to you about college."

"Yeah, and I told her I didn't want to go straight out of high school."

"I know, but we still have to discuss this with her. She needs to be on the same page. And there'd be a ton of rules you'd have to follow. I don't care if you're eighteen and an adult; I'm not helping you get on the tour unless you agree to my rules."

"Fine by me," I say without zero hesitation because I want this more than anything.

"All right, we'll discuss them after we talk to your mom and your band. Ayden might be a little tricky, considering everything that's going on, but maybe if I talk to Ethan, it might help get everyone to agree to let him go."

"Thank you. Thank you. Thank you." I pull away, beaming from ear to ear. "I'm going to go tell Ayden now and track down Sage and Nolan tomorrow, but I bet they'll be in." I head for the door with a huge smile on my face, but then suddenly remember something. "Hey, Dad. There was a lady at the bar earlier. She said her name was Ava, and she knew you from Wyoming. Did she stop in and say hi?"

"No . . ." His forehead creases. "I'm sorry, but how did you end up talking to this person?"

"She stopped me when I was walking by. I think she recognized me or something." Now that I say it aloud, though, it seems odd. How did she recognize me when I've never met her?

"How did she, though?" He scratches his head. "I don't talk to anyone who still lives there except your grandma and grandpa."

"Maybe they're the ones who showed her a picture of me or something."

"Did she give a last name?"

"No, she didn't give me a last name. She was around Mom's age."

"Are you sure it wasn't your mother?" he jokes, still edgy.

"Ha, ha, you're a freaking riot, old man." I wrap my fingers around the doorknob. "No, it wasn't Mom. She had blonde hair and these really blue eyes."

He rubs his scruffy jawline, seeming baffled. "Do me a

favor and go straight home with Ayden until I can find out who she is."

"Should I be worried?" I ask, opening the door.

He pushes back from the desk and rises to his feet, stretching out his legs. "I'm not sure, but the best thing to do is be safe."

The excitement over the tour gradually fades as my dad follows me out of his office. We check around the floor area and the bar for the woman, but she's nowhere to been seen. So, he walks me to Ayden's car and sends us on our way after we promise to drive straight home and nowhere else.

"I'm sorry we don't get to go to the bridge," I tell Ayden as he steers the car down the busy road toward our neighborhood.

Lampposts reflect in the cab and shimmer across his face as we pass by stores, houses, and people strolling up and down the sidewalks, the city alive and awake.

"It's okay." He shrugs it off as he shifts gears. The rainstorm has cleared, but the roads are wet, and puddles splash against the tires. "I get why your dad's worried. I just wish I could have seen this woman myself."

"Why?"

"Because . . . Maybe I would have recognized her. Maybe that's why I felt uncomfortable on stage. I could sense I was being watched."

"You think she might know the people who . . . ?" I nervously bite on my fingernails.

"I don't know. At this point, I'm starting to question every person I pass by on the street." He taps on the brakes to stop at a light.

"We should find something relaxing for you to do tonight." I reach for his hand.

"Like what?" Interest lights up in his eyes.

"I don't know . . . We could drink some more champagne if we can steal a bottle from the fridge. And then we could hang out in the hot tub. The damn thing never gets used, and it's supposed to be relaxing, right?"

His eyes enlarge, and I remember why we never use the hot tub. Ayden can barely stand being shirtless in front of anyone, which leaves water activities out of the picture.

"Never mind. Let me think of something cooler."

"No . . ." His fingers twitch against mine. "I mean, we can try it. I'm supposed to be trying new things, anyway."

"Says who?"

"Says my therapist."

"All right, if you're okay with it, then let's do it." I raise my knuckles for a fist bump.

Ayden laughs, but taps his knuckles against mine.

"What else did you want to tell me?" he asks as he drives forward through an intersection. "When you came out to the car with your dad, you said there was some awesome news you needed to tell me."

"Oh, it's more than awesome news, but I'm going to make you wait until we get home. Build the anticipation." I prop my feet up on the dashboard and tip my head to the side to stare out the window at the stars peeking through the clouds.

I don't know how many times I've gazed up at them, making wish after wish that I'd one day get to live out my dream of being a singer. I never really thought they'd grant me my wish.

Stars, stars, shining above,

I've whispered to you

So many times,

Told you my secrets

And sold you my soul

In exchange for guidance.

Stars, stars, shining above,

I'll tell you another

Wish from the heart

Then close my eyes

And blow out the light

And wait for you in the dark.

Chapter 11

Lyric

About a half an hour later, I'm sitting on the edge of the empty hot tub out in my backyard, wearing my favorite black bikini. Apparently, because no one ever uses the hot tub, my parents drained it. Since I have no clue how to fill it, I sit with my feet inside, trying to figure out what to do. My mom is working late at the gallery, so I was able to steal two beers from the fridge—my parents aren't really champagne kind of people.

Ayden went inside his house about ten minutes ago to get changed into some shorts. Honestly, I'm not one hundred percent sure he's going to come out, not when he thinks we're going to get into the water and he's going to have to strip off his shirt in order to do that.

The hot tub has a stereo built into it, so I mess around until I find the perfect song, "The Ocean" by Manchester

Orchestra. Then I pop the top off the beer, sit back, and wait, hoping I don't have to wait forever.

Two minutes later, my phone buzzes from beside me. Figuring it's Ayden, I pick it up, preparing to read a rejection on my hot tub offer. Instead, the message is from Maggie, a friend from school.

Maggie: I thought u said u were coming to my party.

Me: I said I would try, but some stuff came up.

Maggie: U mean sexy goth boy stuff?

Me: Yeah, sort of.

Maggie: U can bring him.

No, I really can't. With all the drama going on, there's no way Ayden's parents will let him go party it up without parental supervision.

Me: Sorry, we're already busy.

Maggie: Now, I like the sound of that. It's about time u two bumped uglies, just like I'm about to bump uglies with Sage.

Me: Okay, first off, bump uglies? Seriously? That's what you call it? Secondly, Ayden and I aren't having sex. We're just hanging out in my backyard. And third-

ly, Sage???? WTF?

Maggie: What? He's hot.

Me: Yeah, but you two hate each other.

Maggie: There's a thin line between love and hate.

Me: Not really.

Maggie. Oh, whatever. Sage is hot, and if I want to fuck him, I can.

Me: Sorry. You're right. I didn't mean to sound so bitchy.

Maggie: Apology accepted. Now, let's get back to you and Ayden not having sex. Why the hell not?

Me: Because we're not ready.

Not entirely true. Sometimes, I feel like I am ready, but I know for a fact Ayden isn't.

Maggie: Yeah, right. So is it u or him? I'm guessing him since u asked me last week what it was like.

I scrunch my nose at her message and consider putting my phone away.

In a moment of sheer curiosity, I asked her about sex. Not because I'm clueless. I just wanted to know firsthand how bad it hurt in case, one day in the far, far, far away future, Ayden and I end up having sex.

Me: Hey, I have to go. My parents need me.

I put the phone down on the brim of the hot tub. It buzzes a few more times before Maggie gives up. I'm not upset with her or anything. It just doesn't feel right discussing my and Ayden's relationship with her when she doesn't have a clue what's going on with him, and it's really none of her business.

A half a beer later, Ayden finally wanders into my backyard. He's wearing a pair of black board shorts and a green T-shirt. His black hair is damp and hangs in his eyes.

"Did you shower?" I lean forward to get a better look at him.

He ruffles his damp hair into place. "Yeah, I wanted to wash the rain out of my hair." He hoists himself up beside me, plants his bare feet into the empty hot tub, and discreetly but thoroughly checks out my body. Then his gaze drops to our feet. "What the hell? Where's the water?"

"Yeah, so apparently, my parents drained it because no one ever uses it." I hand him a beer. "I did manage to steal a couple of these, though."

"So, what do we do now, then?" He pops the top off the beer and slants his head back to take a swallow.

I stare at the sad, pathetic excuse for a hot tub. "Do

you know how to fill it?"

He shakes his head. "I've never even been in a hot tub before."

"Not even back when . . ." I bite my lips to stop myself from mentioning his past.

"Back when I lived with my birth mother?" he asks, scratching the back of his neck. "It's okay, you can ask me stuff if you want to. I've been working on it in therapy . . . I mean, with that kind of stuff."

"Like hot tub stuff?"

"Yeah, like hot tub stuff." He scoots toward me until our knees are touching.

I stifle a smile because I can tell he did it on purpose, needing to touch me.

"And to answer your question," he says. "My birth mother wasn't really the take-her-kids-swimming type, and that includes hot tubs."

"So, what did you do for fun, then?" I swallow a little bit more beer then balance the bottle between my legs.

"Get into trouble." He gives a half-shrug. "You remember what I looked like when we met, right? That was basically who I was for the longest time."

"What do you mean by trouble, exactly? I know you

drank, smoked, and got into fights, but any arrests I need to know about?" I dazzle him with a smile so he'll know I'm messing with him.

"No, no arrests." He relaxes back and stares up at the sky while sipping his beer. "My mother wasn't a good mother, and you already know that I didn't know my dad, so basically, my brother . . . my sister, and me just ran wild from the day we were born. We got into a ton of trouble all the time and did a lot of shitty stuff. Sometimes, I worry it's all going to catch up with me."

"My dad doesn't really know his dad, either. I guess he left his family when he was like six and started a new family. And, from what I understand, my mother's parents were neglectful, although my grandpa turned his life around."

When he looks at me in puzzlement, I get to the point. "What I'm trying to say is that, from some of the stories I've heard over the years, they got into a *ton* of trouble, but they turned out just fine. For parents, they're actually pretty cool." I clink bottles with him. "So, I'm betting you'll turn out just fine. In fact, you kind of already have."

"I still have a long ways to go before I'm fine, but I'll admit that I'm getting better."

My jaw drops in mock shock as I place my hand over my mouth. "Did you just say something nice about yourself, Shy Boy?"

His lips quirk. "Maybe."

I grin like I've just won the freaking lottery. "You should do it more often."

He remains quiet as he gazes at the night sky. Most of the clouds have thinned, and the stars and moon glimmer vibrantly above us.

"So, you want to hear my news?" I ask abruptly. "Because it's pretty big and epic."

His head cocks to the side as his attention falls to me. "Let's hear it."

Unable to conceal my enthusiasm any longer, an absurdly huge smile takes over my face. "It's about the band and a tour."

"*Really*? What one?"

"I think it's called the Rocking Summer Blast Tour or something like that. I have a paper in my room about it. My dad actually got us the gig, and it's not the biggest, most popular line-up, but it could help us get a foot in the door. Plus, imagine how cool it would be. You and me on the road, twenty-four seven, singing and writing lyrics while we see the country. We could have this super awesome duet at the end of our performance." When he doesn't say anything right away, I add, "Isn't it exciting?"

He doesn't seem that excited, more like disappointed. "I'm not sure if I can go . . . not when my sister's still out there."

I have no idea what to say to that. Honestly, I don't think there's anything I can say. He's clearly suffering over his sister, and I'm not about to try to convince him he's wrong for feeling that way.

"What can I do to help?"

He shrugs. "There's nothing anyone can do except wait for the police to find her." He grows quiet for a minute, studying the scars on the back of his hands. "Sometimes, I think about going to look for her myself"—he stares across the yard at his house—"tracking down every place connected to their name and seeing if she's being held at any of them."

My expression plummets. "I think you should just let the police do their job."

"I'm not saying I'm going to. I was just telling you I think about it sometimes."

"When you think about doing stuff, you usually do it." My sharp tone surprises me, almost as much as how afraid I am that he's going to actually go through with what he said.

He jerks back, thrown off by outburst. "No, I don't . . . I was just telling you because"—hurt masks his expression—"I thought that's what we did."

"Yeah, we do." I swing my legs out of the hot tub, hop down onto the grass, and cross my arms, staring him down. "But you keep doing things like tracking that hacker down and going to that house, so when you say things like you're going to go track down these places, I get worried you're actually going to do it."

"I'm not going to go looking for them. I just need to do"—he balls his hands into fists, staring above us, as if cursing the stars—"something. I'm so sick of waiting around until they finally decide to take me. Like today at the concert. I was fine until I was around a bunch of people. Then all I kept thinking is how someone could be watching me in the audience, waiting to make their next move, just like they did to Sadie. Did you know they kidnapped her right out of her home?"

"They're not going to take you!" I shout, startling the both of us. I try to calm myself down, but it's like there are these waves inside me, roaring and swirling, and I feel like I'm drowning in the center of it. "Nothing's going to happen to you, and you're not going to go look for these places. Promise me you won't do it. Ever."

His eyes widen as he gapes at me in horror. That's when I realize tears are pouring from my eyes and down my cheeks. We hardly ever fight—I hardly ever fight with anyone—but the idea of him doing something stupid that could potentially lead to me losing him is making me feel like I'm losing my damn mind.

I can't ever lose him.
Ever. Ever. Ever.
Let the ocean take me away and drown me
in rage.
I'll give myself away,
Just as long he stays safe.
And never, ever goes away.

"Lyric, I get that you're upset, but—"

"No, you don't get it," I cut him off, sounding calmer. "You don't care about yourself, so I don't think you realize how much it would kill me if something happened to you, because you don't think someone can care about you that much. But I care about you that much."

"It wouldn't kill—"

"I love you." Probably the worst moment ever to say it, but what's done is done and I'm not going to take it back. Honestly, I kind of feel better, like I got a few tiny rays of sunshine back.

I step toward him, feeling calm as a summer day. "If you care about me at all, you'll promise you won't go looking for these places, and you'll let the police do it." I lift my hand and hitch my pinkie toward him. "In fact, you'll pinkie swear on it."

He opens his mouth in a protest, but then his jaw snaps shut. He does the movement repeatedly, as if I shocked his voice right out of him. Then he searches my eyes for something with his face contorted in puzzlement.

"All right," he finally says as he loops his pinkie with mine. "I pinkie swear I won't go look for the places and will just talk to the police about it."

I suck back my tears. "Good."

A moment or two drifts by before we pull away. Another handful of seconds tick by before anyone says anything.

"Can I kiss you and make it better?" He chews on his

bottom lip, mulling something over. "I don't like seeing you cry, especially when I'm the one who caused it."

I dry my tears from my cheeks then nod, and he seals his lips to mine, giving me the softest kiss.

The longer we kiss under the stars, the more I feel at peace. It doesn't matter if he didn't say I love you back. I wasn't expecting him to. I just needed to let him know how much I care about him, and I think I did exactly that.

Besides, deep down, in his own way, I think he might love me. I can tell through his little touches, kisses, smiles, and how he agreed to do something tonight that he didn't really want to do, but felt he needed to because he didn't want to see me hurt.

Words are just words
That pass across lips.
Actions show more
Than words ever can understand.
Ayden's actions are beautiful,
And tell me all I need to know,
Feed my soul and give me hope.

"What can I do to make tonight up to you?" he asks when we finally come up for air.

"You don't need to make anything up to me." I hitch my arms around him. "We had our first fight. So what? It was bound to happen sometime."

"Okay, then what should we do to celebrate"—he glances at the hot tub—"because I think sitting in the hot tub is off the table."

I thrum my finger against my lip. "I have an idea."

He eyes me over with suspicion. "You have that look in your eye."

"What look?" I bat my eyelashes innocently.

He gives me a blank stare. "The look that means you're about to get us into trouble."

"I promise we won't get in trouble. You might not be too thrilled about it, though."

Before he can press for more details, I snatch ahold of his hand and drag him toward his house.

As we're rounding the fence, I notice a maroon SUV parked in front of his house.

"So, that's the infamous detective?" I smile at the car and give a little wave.

"You're such a weirdo," he jokes then steers me toward the backdoor of his house.

The alarm goes off when we enter, and he hurries

through the darkness to turn it off. I flip on the lights and bend down to untie my boots.

I feel him move up behind me before I actually see him.

"Hey." I stand upright, my back aligning with his chest.

As he circles his arms around my waist, the air feels electric, sharp zaps biting at my skin.

He rests his chin on my shoulder. "So, what did you want to do?"

"I was thinking we could work on that song we've been writing . . . and you could sing it for me."

"I knew you were up to something, but I already told you I can't sing."

"I'll be the one to decide that." I start to turn around to head for the kitchen, but he tightens his hold on me.

"Are you sure that's what you want to do?" There's a playfulness to his voice that's got me really curious where he's going with this.

"Yeah, you kind of owe me." It's a lie. He doesn't owe me anything, but I really want to hear him sing.

"Oh, yeah?" His lips dip toward my neck. "How do

you figure?"

"Becausc you . . ." My eyes roll back, and my knees almost buckle as he sucks on the side of my neck.

The harder he sucks, the more difficult it becomes to keep my legs under me. Fortunately, he has his arms around me and keeps me from toppling to the ground.

"You sure you still want to hear me sing?" His warm breath falters against my neck. "Because I could . . . I could keep doing this."

After I regain my breath, I glare at him from over my shoulder. "Don't try to play me like a sucker. I know you're trying to distract me, and it's not going to work." I slip out from under his arms and grab his hand. "Now, get your ass upstairs and sing for me so I can see if I'm ever going to be able to live out my dream of doing a duet with you." I haul him toward the kitchen, giving a playful glance over my shoulder. "And, when we're done, you can suck on my neck some more as punishment for trying to play me."

"I'm all for the sucking on the neck part, but don't say I didn't warn you about the singing thing."

"Let me be the judge of that."

Even though I have no clue what his singing voice

sounds like, the dreamer side of me believes it's going to be low and smooth, like honey, and absolutely, one hundred percent dripping with sexiness. He may not agree with me, but he has zero confidence and doesn't believe anything about him is good.

When we enter his room, I release his hand and cross my arms, refusing to let him off the hook, even when he gives me his sad, puppy dog eyes.

"All right, Shy Boy, show me what you've got."

Chapter 12

Ayden

I love you. She said she *loves* me.

Love. Love. Love.

At first, I thought she was kidding.

I could see on her face that she wasn't, though. I thought about talking her out of it, telling her she really doesn't love me—couldn't—but the longer I stared at her, the more I could see how truthful she was being. There was no way I was going to be able to talk her out of it.

It was that look that made me pinkie swear that I wouldn't go looking for those places. I will keep my word, too, no matter how bad things get, because she's Lyric and I . . .

I, what exactly?

I think deep down I know just how much I care about her.

Enough that I would give up almost anything.

Lyric watches me as I situate on the bed with my guitar on my lap. Her eyes are lit up with anticipation that my voice is going to sound amazing, and I feel bad that, in a moment, I'm going to let her down.

"Are you sure you want me to do this?" I ask, lining my fingers along the strings. "Because, once I sing, there's no going back. That dream of yours will forever be crushed."

She bounces down on the foot of the bed. "Just do it, Shy Boy." She snaps her fingers impatiently. "Stop procrastinating."

She's still wearing her bikini, and the sight of her skin and curves is a nice distraction from the fact that I'm about to sing in front of someone for the very first time.

"All right, but don't say I didn't warn you." I lean back against the headboard and think of which song to play. My instinct tells me to go with a cover song, but then I figure, if I'm doing this, I might as well go all the way and sing one of my own songs.

As I open my mouth, I have no idea which song is going to come out.

"Stuck in the dust
Of a soul that was crushed,
I silently bleed in the stillness.
Aching inside, most days I feel like I'm losing my mind.
I'm dying inside.
And no one can help me."

I play a few more chords as I sing the chorus.

"Stuck in a sea of pain,
I thought nothing would ever change,
That my life would always be this way."

My fingers strum the strings.

"You blindsided me out of nowhere,
Right when I was about to surrender to the darkness,
Swallow it down with a handful of pills and sink to the bottom of the water.
Take away the pain so I can't feel it anymore.
So close to the edge,
You offered me your hand and dragged me to the shore."

I stop playing, even though the song isn't finished, because Lyric is crying. Hot tears spill down her cheeks as she hugs her knees to her chest.

"Fuck, I'm sorry." I set my guitar aside and scoot down to the bottom of the bed beside her. "I don't know why I picked that song. I should have sung something different. Something happier."

"Is it true?" More tears stream from her eyes and down her cheeks. "Did you really think about taking your own life?"

I want to lie to her, but she deserves better.

"I used to, but I haven't thought about it since . . . well, since you and I became friends."

"Oh, Ayden, I never knew it was that bad for you." She slides her legs to the side of the bed and throws her arms around me.

"It's not that bad anymore." I breathe in the scent of her as I wrap my arms around her. "I promise."

I close my eyes and breathe in the truth. Yes, there's a ton of bad stuff going on in my life, but the darkness that used to grasp me by the ankles and wrists has lightened. The pain isn't so heavy, the scars easier to bear. But, if I'd never met Lyric and the Gregorys, I'm not sure I would have ever made it here to this moment.

"Your voice is beautiful, by the way," she whispers. "Even better than I thought it was going to be, so now you have no more excuses not to sing with me."

I want to argue with her, tell her she's wrong. My voice isn't beautiful. I can't sing with her. Instead, I decide to nod and enjoy the moment I almost didn't have.

Chapter 13

Ayden

The week is fairly uneventful, maybe even a little on the normal side. By Friday, I no longer have a detective tailing my every move. I make sure to do everything I'm supposed to and don't wander off. My life consists of school, band practice, therapy, family time, and Lyric.

Lyric, Lyric, Lyric. I spend all my free time with her, yet it still never feels like enough. I don't know what's happening to me exactly, but something is definitely changing.

"Knock. Knock. Knock." Lyric raps her hand on the doorframe as she strolls into my bedroom with her sketchbook tucked under her arm. She's wearing a short purple dress, her leather jacket, and black platforms. Her hair is wild around her face, and her lips are stained pink and look absurdly tempting. "Happy tattoo day, Shy Boy."

I prop my guitar against the wall, swing my legs over the edge, and stand to my feet. “Did you finish up the sketch?”

She bobs her head up and down enthusiastically. “I did. You want to see it?”

“Of course.” I reach to take the sketchbook, but she dodges out of my reach.

A slow, conniving grin spreads across her face. “It’ll cost you.”

My arm falls to my side, and my lips twitch with amusement. “What’s the price?”

She taps a finger against her lips. “Let me think about this. Something pretty awesome, of course, since this is a freaking amazing sketch. Not money. Not anything materi-alistic. How about a cookie . . . ? No, that doesn’t seem very awesome. I could always make you do a striptease.”

“Lyric”—laughter bursts from my lips—“just tell me what you want.”

“Oh, fine. Take all the fun out of this.” She fakes a pout, but her smile almost instantly lights up her face again. “It’ll cost you a kiss.”

“That’s it?”

“What can I say? Your kisses are pretty valuable.”

Insert awkwardness on my part. I've never been good with compliments.

"I don't think my kisses are that valuable, but if that's what you want, then I'll give it to you." I step forward, slide my hand around her back, and reel her in for a kiss.

The kiss is quick, but leaves me breathless. When I start to move away, Lyric's arm snakes around my back, and she pushes me right back against her.

"A little bit longer, please," she begs, arching her chest toward me.

I easily give her what she asks and slip my tongue inside her mouth, kissing her the way she deserves. The kiss goes on for seconds, minutes, hours . . . so long I lose track of time.

Out of breath, I finally have to pull away, giving her bottom lip a gentle nip. She shudders in my arms, and I nearly stop breathing.

God, how can I be alive when my heart is beating so quickly?

"Okay, that definitely earned you the reward of seeing this." Her voice is gravelly. She clears her throat before opening the sketchbook and hands it to me. "So, what do you think?"

Lines trace the pages and form shapes and swirls, dark and bright shades and vivid colors, patterns that all surround a fiery gold and red bird with its wings spread wide.

God, this must have taken her forever.

"It's a phoenix," she explains, "which is supposed to mean rebirth and strength. I thought it was pretty fitting."

That's how she sees me? For some reason, the thought causes my heart to swell inside my chest.

I smooth my hand over the page. "It's amazing. More than amazing. I don't even know what to say."

"So, you like it?"

"It's perfect. I don't think you could have done anything more perfect." I shake my head in awe. "God, Lyric, this is amazing. I mean, I know you're talented, but . . . This must have taken you days to draw."

"Nah, it didn't take that long." She waves me off. "But I was freaking out that you would hate it."

"No, I love it." *I love you.* I shake the thought from my head and thank her by kissing her again.

"Oh, a bonus payment." Her lips move against mine as she cracks a joke.

"You can have as many bonus payments as you want. I

owe you a ton, anyway, for putting up with my shit the other night. I should have never upset you like that. I didn't realize that you . . ." I kiss her again and again, tipping her head back and tangling our tongues, her lips hot and inviting.

Moaning, she grips at my arms and clutches onto me as I lower her to the bed.

"As much as I love where this is going," she murmurs as her back is just about to touch the mattress, "on my way up here, I was told to make sure to tell you that we have to leave in no less than five minutes; otherwise, we'll be late for your appointment."

I grunt in response, and she erupts with laughter.

"I've never heard you sound that frustrated before. That was pretty funny."

"You think that's funny?" My hand skates around to her ribcage, and I tickle her.

"Hey!" she gripes, writhing below me. "That's not fair."

"How do you figure?" I tickle her again, secretly loving how her hips thrust against mine every time she moves.

"Because I just gave you the most awesomest sketch of

a tattoo ever. That definitely earns me a no-tickling-for-a-while pass."

"Oh, fine." I tickle her a few more times then push off her and offer my hand.

"Are you nervous?" she asks as I pull her to her feet.

"Yeah," I admit with a shaky breath.

"Don't worry, I've heard it can be more of a high than painful," she says as I slip on my boots.

"I'm not worried about the pain. Pain's fine." I rake my fingers through my hair as we head out of my room and toward the stairs. "I'm just worried about, you know"—I gesture at my side—"my shirt pulled up and someone being that close to me and touching me. What if I freak out or something?"

"That's why I'm going with you," she reminds me as we reach the bottom of the stairs. "I'll hold your hand and keep you so entertained with my charming personality that you'll barely pay attention to anything else. I've even been saving up some juicy gossip for this particular occasion."

"Since when do you gossip?"

"Since this morning when all hell broke loose at the Scott's home."

I bend over to lace my boot. "Is everything all right?"

"It will be as soon as the drama passes."

"You guys ready to go?" Ethan asks as he strolls into the kitchen, swinging the car keys around his finger.

"Surely-durely," Lyric singsongs. When I stand upright, she grabs my hand and jerks me toward the door. "Come on, let's go get the past taken off you."

Twenty minutes later, Ethan is parking the car near the side of town that is enclosed by small shops and restaurants. Ethan owns the one on the corner, a few blocks down from the tattoo shop.

Inside, the windows and walls are decorated with different drawings and images, and in the center of the room is a display case. In the back corner is a curtain, and I can hear a needle buzzing from behind it.

Ethan starts chatting with his buddy, Cole, whose arms and neck are covered with ink.

"Is it doable?" Ethan asks as Cole studies Lyric's sketch.

"It'll definitely take a couple of sessions." He examines the drawing closely then looks at me. "Can I see the tattoo you have now? I just want to make sure this will cover it up."

I glance at Lyric, who gives me an encouraging smile, then step forward and lift up my shirt, revealing the inked patterns that form a jagged circle along my scarred skin.

Cole bends over and squints at the tat. "Whoa, that is probably one of the worst tattoo jobs I've ever seen." He stands upright and frowns at Ethan. "On the phone, you said it was homemade, but I didn't think it would be that bad."

"So, you can't fix it?" Ethan asks, casting a concerned glance in my direction.

My muscles ravel into knots. All this time, I was so focused on getting the actual tattoo that I didn't even consider it might not be able to be covered up. The idea of having it on my body forever sends my stomach dropping.

Cole rubs his jawline. "I didn't say that. I just said I didn't expect it to be that bad." He lowers his hand. "I can cover it up, but the raised scarring will still be there."

"That's fine," Ethan says, crossing his arms. "We didn't expect you to be able to cover up all the scars. We just don't want to be able to see any of the ink that's already there."

"Well, then that works." He looks at the drawing again

as he backs up toward the curtain. “Let me go get this drawn up, and then we’ll go from there.”

“You going to be okay?” Ethan turns to me after Cole disappears through the curtain.

I sink into a chair near the front door. “Yeah, I’m just a little nervous.”

“That’s understandable. If you need anything, just say so, okay?”

I nod, and he stuffs his hands into his pockets then wanders off to look at the framed sketches on the wall.

I lower my head, rest my arms on my knees, and take a few measured breaths, trying to calm myself down.

Lyric plops down beside me and nudges my boot with her foot. “So, I learned interesting stuff today.”

“About your family?” I raise my head up to look at her.

She shakes her head. “Nah, I’m saving that juicy story for when you’re actually getting the tattoo. But this story is mildly entertaining. It’s about Sage and Maggie.”

My brows dip. “I thought they hated each other.”

“Well, apparently, there’s a thin line between love and hate, or so I’ve been told. And they fooled around at a party a while ago." She tucks a lock of her hair behind her ear. "Sage told me about it today in class, which FYI, I think he's starting to see me as a dude. He kept giving me all the details about Maggie's hot body, which I so didn't want to hear."

I laugh because she's so far from wrong. "He doesn't see you as a dude. He's probably just trying to make you jealous."

She rolls her eyes. "No way. I can tell he's over me. He even asked for her number."

"Sage asked for someone's number? He's always telling me he doesn't do relationships." Unless he could have Lyric, which I still think is what his behavior is all about.

"Apparently, he changed his mind. It's kind of funny, though. The two of them hook up with more people than I can count. They almost seem perfect for each other in this weird, sick, whore-ish way."

"I don't know . . . It kind of sounds like a disaster to me. I mean, neither of them have ever been in a relationship for more than a minute." And I still don't believe this is about Maggie.

"True, but I have hope."

"That's because you're you."

She smiles at that. “I am pretty amazing.”

“Yes, you are.” I stretch my legs out. “So, have you told Sage and Nolan about the tour?”

She hesitates then shakes her head. “Not yet.”

“Why not?”

She crosses her legs and reclines back in the chair. “Because I’m waiting for you to agree to go.”

“Lyric—” I start.

“My dad said we have until after we record our album. I’m giving you until then to decide. If you want to go, then I’ll tell Sage and Nolan.”

“I’m not going to—”

She covers my mouth with her hand. “I’m not asking you for an answer right now, so don’t give me one.” She lowers her hand and sits back in the chair. “Give it a few weeks, and then you can tell me your answer.”

I puff out a breath. “Fine.”

But, unless my sister’s found, I won’t go. I can’t take off, hit the road, and live an amazing life while I know Sadie is trapped in darkness somewhere.

For the next twenty minutes or so, Lyric and I chat about lighter things, like the song she’s decided we’re going to sing together. Listening to the sound of her voice and watching her talk animatedly, I fall into another world filled with ease and calmness. But the moment Cole walks out from the curtain, the bubble around us pops.

"Come on back, and let's get this put on you," he says with a nod of his head.

My knees shake as I stand up and cross the room. When Lyric laces our fingers together, I feel the slightest bit better, until Cole tells me to take off my shirt so he can put the sketching on my skin and make sure we get it in the right place before we start.

I glance between Cole, Ethan, and Lyric, knowing I have to do this since the tattoo is on my side, but knowing doesn't make it any easier.

"I can step out if you want me to," Lyric whispers softly enough so only I hear her.

She's never seen me with my shirt off, but if I'm going to have her in here with me while I get the tattoo, then it's going to have to happen. I guess it's time to rip the band-aid off and get over one of my biggest fears. Having her here while I get the tattoo was my decision. Plus, she loves me, and I need to hold on to that.

"No, you're fine." I take my fiftieth nervous breath of

the day, grab the collar of my shirt, and pull it over my head.

By the time I get it off, my pulse is racing so fast I swear I'm going to have a heart attack. It's the first time anyone has seen me shirtless since I was freed from that house except on a few rare occasions when Lyric walked into my room without knocking. I'm terrified, yet I've made this huge step forward.

Forward, forward, forward.

Please, just let me fly

Instead of falling off the cliff.

Lyric dips her head to catch my gaze. "You okay?"

"Yeah . . . I think so." I cringe at the wobbliness of my voice.

My heart races violently the entire time Cole aligns the drawing on my ribcage. I hope that, by the time I lie down in the chair, I'll relax, but that doesn't end up being the case.

Instead, I become nervous over the needle. I stare at the ceiling, deeply inhaling and exhaling while trying to picture myself in a calm place—near the ocean, in the mountains, all alone. It's a relaxation technique Dr.

Gardingdale taught me, but it doesn't help. By the time the needle pokes my skin, I almost bolt from the chair.

Nails, biting nails,

Scrape layer after layer,

Peel away your soul.

You'll never be the same again.

We'll make sure of that.

You'll be tainted.

I don't want to be tainted. I want to be whole.

I'm stronger than that. I have to be stronger.

Or else what do I have to live for?

"Hey, look at me." Lyric's comforting voice draws me away from my thoughts.

I open my eyes and find her staring down at me.

"Do you want to hear my story now?" she asks in a calm, soothing voice.

As I stare into her bright green eyes, a calm rolls over me. "Yeah, tell me the story."

She smiles, drags a chair over, and sits down beside me, holding my hand. "So, guess who the blond woman at the bar turned out to be?"

I hear the buzzing of the needle, distantly feel it, but

feel her more potently. “Who?”

“My dad’s half-sister.”

“*What*? Where the hell did she come from? I thought your dad was an only child or something.”

“Remember how I told you that he hasn’t had contact with his father or his new family in forever. Well, I guess his half-sister decided she wanted to see him. She recognized me because she saw pictures on the Internet and tracked my dad down that way. I guess she chickened out last weekend, though, after talking to me. Then she showed up at his studio last night.”

“What happened?”

“At first, my dad was irritated and thought she was there because she needed something. But, when he realized she was genuinely there to see him, they chatted for a while. I guess she wants to be part of our lives.”

She props her elbows on the edge of the chair and rests her chin on her hands. “She said she’s wanted to meet him for a while, but she was afraid my dad would be upset with her because their dad’s such a fucking bastard. Plus, we lived so far away that it made it hard to just stop by. Then her husband got transferred to San Diego, and she decided she no longer had an excuse. She has kids, too. I think a daughter and a son. I'm not sure about all the deets, but I guess we're supposed to hang out sometime or something."

"That's so weird . . . that he suddenly has a sister." So weird, but I'm jealous.

The jealously is short-lived, because my skin starts to burn from the needle, and my eyelids start to close as I plummet toward the darkness.

Lyric pulls me right back out, delicately placing her palm on my cheek. "Hey, look at me."

When I open my eyes, my gaze locks with hers. I wait for her to say something, but instead, she intensely carries my gaze. I feel myself falling again, only someplace different. Someplace new.

Feel, feel, feel your heart beating.

It feels so free

With her eyes on you.

Nothing else matters.

Time has vanished.

The past doesn't exist.

The pain and the wrong is gone.

Feel, feel, feel yourself sinking.

Not into the darkness

Where the chains pull you down.

But into the light

Where your heart is waiting to be found.

Found, found, found.

I'm not sure how long I lay in that chair, but it's enough time that my legs are wobbly when I stand. Once I get my footing, I stare at my reflection in the mirror. The outline of the tattoo inks my ribcage. Through the twists, lines, and dark curves of the feather and beak, the scars are still visible, yet I feel lighter inside, different, less bound. I took a massive step today.

Ethan thanks Cole for doing a kickass job then makes me another appointment to get the outlines shaded while I put my shirt back on. Then I leave the back room with Lyric, and we head for the car.

During the drive home, Lyric and I sit in the backseat with our hands clasped. The contact of her skin lulls me into a relaxing state as I lean my head against the window and watch the buildings and houses drift by.

My thoughts drift to Sadie. I wish she could have been here with me, getting her tattoo covered up. I vow to myself that, one day, when she's found, I'll take her to do just that. I'll help her feel free from the darkness like the Gregorys and Lyric have helped me.

Freedom, is that was this is? Have I finally found something I never thought existed? Is it possible that one day I'll be free?

All I can do is hope.

Chapter 14

Lyric

Something changed in Ayden the day he got the outline of his tattoo. He became more at ease, as if the mark on his ribcage had been weighing him down. Don't get me wrong, he's still my shy boy who is holding onto a lot of pain and constantly worries about his sister. But he has been smiling more, which has to be a step forward, right?

A couple of weeks drift by before he goes in to get the shading done. I want to go with him, but the appointment falls on the day my family and I are meeting my father's sister and her husband.

They arrive at the house around five o'clock to have dinner, dressed to impress. Seeing my aunt again, I wonder how I ever could have missed the family resemblance. My father and her share the same blond hair and sky blue eyes and joking mannerism to the point that the relation is almost uncanny.

Around six, we gather around the dinner table to eat. Outside the window, the sun is setting, and next door, the Gregory's driveway is vacant, which means Ayden is still getting his tattoo. As soon as I see that car, though, I'm bailing out to go over there.

"So, where are your kids?" I ask Ava as I pick at my chicken.

"They're actually still back in New York with their grandparents," Ava explains, wrapping her fingers around the wineglass. "We wanted to get settled before we brought them out here."

I wonder if she means with the grandfather I've never met. I don't ask, though, sincc I can tell the subject is making my dad uncomfortable.

"We'll definitely have to bring them over when we get them out here," she continues after taking a sip of wine. "I think you and my oldest would really get along. He's really into music."

Funny, I wonder if my dad got his musical talent from his dad, then.

"Does he play anything?" I ask, scooping up a glob of mash potatoes.

"He plays the cello," her husband, Glen, answers, poking his fork into the salad. "And he used to play the flute when he was younger, but when he reached fourteen, he gave it up. Said he was too old for it."

"I play the violin," I tell them. "Maybe we could rock out sometime, orchestra style. Unless he plays symphonic rock."

"I think I've heard him mention something about that before." He exchanges a look with Ava who shrugs.

"Beats me." She sets the wineglass down. "He goes through a new phase every other week. The only thing he's stuck with is the cello."

"How old is he?" I reach for a roll.

"He's fifteen," Ava replies as my mom refills her glass with wine.

"So, Kale's age," I remark. "Sounds about right."

Kale goes through phases like no other. Like that girl he had a crush on a month ago. He's moved on from her and is already focused on someone else.

"Who's Kale?" Ava wonders, picking up the glass again.

I open my mouth to reply, but I see headlights pull into

the Gregory's driveway and turn to my mother. "Ayden's home. Can I go over and see how everything turned out?"

She glances at Ava and her husband then starts to protest, but Ava interrupts.

"Don't keep her here on our part." She winks at me, reminding me so much of my dad it's weird. "We have plenty of time to catch up."

"Fine. Go." My mom gets up to gather the dishes as I push back from the table. "You should tell Lila and Ethan to come over later and chat for a while." Chat is code for drink wine and reminisce about the good ol' days.

Nodding, I take my dishes to the sink and rinse them off then hurry for the back door.

"Don't stay too late," my mom calls out as I step outside. "And make sure to keep Ayden's door open."

"Okay!" I roll my eyes then shut the door and jump the fence.

I walk in without knocking, a bad habit of mine. Aunt Lila and Uncle Ethan are in the kitchen, chatting about something.

"Hey," Aunt Lila greets me when I close the back door. "How'd everything go with the family dinner?"

"It seems to be going okay, but that's usually the case

when wine is involved." I slip my sandals off and walk into the kitchen. "They said you two should go over and chat for a while."

"I think we could do that for a bit, right?" Lila says to Ethan. "It is the weekend, and no one has practice or anything."

He shrugs as he moves for the cupboard. "It's fine by me. I'm not working this weekend."

"Is Ayden upstairs?" I ask, walking backwards for the stairway.

"He is." Lila eyes me warily from across the kitchen. "If you go up there, you better make sure you keep that door open."

"My mother said the exact same thing." I pause at the bottom step. "How'd his tattoo go?"

"He seems okay," Ethan answers, opening the fridge. "I think he handled it better when you were there, but he still did pretty okay today."

Ethan's version of okay can be a little iffy since he's fine with almost everything.

Without saying anything else, I turn around and trot up the stairs. When I reach Ayden's closed bedroom door, I knock as I walk in, something I've done since the day we met.

He's sitting on his bed, writing in his journal with his leg stretched out and his back propped against the headboard.

"Hey," he says, smiling at me.

"Whatcha doing?" I plop down on the bed beside him, roll on my side, and prop up on my elbow.

"Just writing about what happened today." He closes the journal, tosses it on the nightstand, and lies down facing me. "About how good it felt to get that damn mark all covered up."

"Hey, we're going over to your house for a little while." Lila pokes her head in, suspicion crossing her face as she eyes Ayden and me on the bed. "Would you two mind sitting on the floor?"

Ayden sighs but climbs off the bed, and I begrudgingly follow. He takes a seat in his computer chair, and I sit down on the trunk near the foot of his bed.

"Everson and Kale are sleeping over at a friend's house," she informs us. "And Fiona is downstairs in the den watching some weird documentary about psychics. Keep an eye on her, please, and keep this door open at all times."

She pushes the door open all the way before backing toward the hall. "I'm going to set the alarm, but if you need anything at all, we're right next door. We shouldn't be long." She steps back, pushing on the door again, even though it's already open to the wall.

"They'll be gone for more than a while," I say once I hear the front door shut. "Ava and her husband are there, and you know how chatty Aunt Lila is with new people. Plus, they have the wine out."

Ayden chuckles as he spins the chair from side to side. "That's okay. They should enjoy themselves. I think I put a lot of stress on them today."

"So, how did today go?" I ask, leaning back on my hands.

"Okay." He rakes his fingers through his hair. "I mean, it would have been better if you were there, but I made it through it and feel pretty good right now."

"Can I . . . ?" I bite down on my lip, wondering if I should ask.

"Can you what?" he wonders with his forehead creased.

I let my lip pop free. "Can I see the tattoo?"

He hesitates before his fingers drift toward the bottom of his dark grey T-shirt. “Yeah, sure.”

“Are you sure?” I double check. “You don’t have to show me if you don’t want to.”

“No . . . I want to.” He grips the fabric. “Besides, you should get to see your artwork.” Summoning a deep inhale, he lifts the shirt up and slips one arm out of the sleeve.

Bright red and gold ink splatters up his side along with intricate shades that contrast with the dark lines of the feathers and cover the mark.

“It’s gorgeous.” *You’re gorgeous.* “Cole did an amazing job.” I climb off the trunk and move in front of Ayden to get a better look. “Man, I so need to get a tattoo.” Instinctively, I reach forward to touch him, but realize he’s probably not going to like that, so I pull back.

Ayden catches my hand. “I want to try something,” he whispers, his voice strained.

I nod, even though I don’t have a damn clue what he’s about to do. Don’t care, though. Let him do whatever he wants with me.

He slowly guides my hand back to him and, with an uneven breath, places my palm on his chest. His heart is hammering and slams against my hand.

I don't say anything. I can barely breathe, knowing how significant this moment is to him—to us.

"Your skin's so soft," I utter, afraid to move my hand and ruin the moment.

His hands slide to my hips, and his fingers inch up my shirt. "So's yours." He traces his finger back and forth along the speck of flesh.

A shiver courses through me, and I suddenly can't breathe.

Air ripped from my lungs.

Heart bleeding.

I need to see all of him,

Every inch,

Feel the softness of him against me.

I want it so badly my soul aches.

I start to draw back because it seems like we could both use a break from the intensity, but my hands have other ideas, and my fingers drift up his chest. When he doesn't protest, I inch my hand higher, keeping our eyes locked, making sure he's all right. I don't want to push him. If he so much as even looks like he's freaking out, I'll stop in a heartbeat.

When his eyes snap wide, I jerk back. “Sorry.”

“No, it’s fine.” He counts to three under his breath then, with a swift yank, removes his shirt. “I want to . . .” His breath falters as I take in the sight of him.

While he was getting his tattoo, I tried my best not to stare. Right now, all I do is stare. Stare, stare, stare forever. He’s not ripped like a jock or sculpted like a model. He’s lean and toned and has a few scars on his skin. He’s the most perfect thing I’ve ever laid eyes on, and it almost makes me cry that he’s mine.

“You’re so beautiful.” I gently place my hands on his chest and his skin feels warm against my palms.

He shivers from my touch. “I want to feel you, too”—he takes a few shallow breaths—“against me.”

I want to ask him if he can handle that, but I don’t think he’d ask if he didn’t actually want to. And I want to, too. So, so much, I can hardly stand it.

I step back and shut the door. Then I head back across the room toward him, lifting my shirt over my head.

His grey eyes soak me in as I fumble with the clasp of my bra. Once unfastened, I lower the straps from my shoulders and toss it on the floor. Then I turn to his iPod on the dresser, scroll to my playlist, and select “Youth” by

Daughter.

"This seems like the kind of moment that needs a song," I explain when he gives me a puzzled look.

As I climb up on his lap and put a leg on either side of him, he struggles to breathe evenly, and my heart slams against my chest. He's nervous. I'm nervous. This isn't a big deal just for him. I've never been this far with a guy before, and I'm glad Ayden is my first. Glad I get to experience a lot of my firsts with him.

He smooths his hands over my sides as I loop my arms around his neck and press my chest against his. The skin-to-skin contact is better than I could have ever imagined in my crazy, imaginative mind.

He's warm enough to thaw a thousand ice-
bergs,
Liquefy the world into water,
Melt the coldest of hearts,
Chip away at frigid souls.

He gasps as I clutch onto him. Then he slips his arms around me, presses me closer, and buries his head in the crook of my neck, kissing my hammering pulse.

A few tears land on my shoulder as he starts to cry.

"I love you," I whisper just loud enough for him to hear.

He doesn't say it back, but he embraces me with everything he has in him, and I know it's his silent way of saying it back.

Chapter 15

Ayden

Saturday night might have been one of the most amazing nights I've ever had. Spending the night with Lyric in my arms, simply holding each other with our bodies connected, surpassed every good experience. She said I love you again, and I almost said it back.

The words burned on the tip of my tongue,
Scorching metal,
Ready to brand our souls
Forever.

I didn't quite make it there, but I'm not too upset with myself. In fact, I'm probably the happiest I've been in a long time.

All that changes Monday morning when I open the car door to go to school. In the center of the driver's seat is a piece of paper wrapped by a faded pink ribbon.

~~Knife~~

~~Hair~~

~~Sadie~~

Sacrifice.

It's time we finally talked, Ayden. Meet us as the Golden Center Docks tonight at 10:00 if you ever want to see you sister again. And make sure to come alone.

"Sadie," I whisper, my hand trembling as I tumble into a memory.

"Ayden, help me!" she cries through the darkness.

I can't see her anywhere.

Where is she? Where is she? Where is she?

I search the darkness and see a woman with blood red hair.

Red hair, like blood.

Then I see Sadie chained to a wall, her pink ribbon stained with drops of blood.

"We're always watching you."

I blink from the memory, my body quivering as I jerk my hand back. I can't touch it, not when there might be fingerprints.

My gaze skims the neighborhood, searching for a face

I can't remember. Since it's early May, the neighborhood is buzzing with the summer air, and people seem to be everywhere. Short, tall, thin, heavy, a guy with blonde hair, a woman with red hair, and it feels as if they're all watching me.

Blood, blood, blood everywhere.

Red nails.

Red hair.

Blood, blood, blood.

I run up the driveway to the house, throw open the back door, and stumble into the kitchen.

"Ayden." Lila's head snaps up from her breakfast, and her eyes widen as she shoves the chair back from the table. "Oh, my God, what happened?"

"A letter," I barely get the words out as I point at the back door. "There's a letter on the seat of the car."

Ethan is storming for the back door in less time than it takes me to suck in my next breath. "Stay here," he warns as he rushes outside, slamming the door behind him.

Lila hurries over around the table to me as I sink down in a chair.

"The note . . ." I lower my head into my hands, guilt

crushing my chest. “It had my sister’s hair ribbon on it . . . It had to be hers.”

Lila kneels down in front of me and folds her arms around me. “Everything’s going to be okay.”

Five minutes ago, I would have agreed with her.

“No, it’s not,” I croak. “The note said that, if I want to see my sister again, I have to meet them at the Golden Center Docks tonight.”

“Don’t worry. That’s not going to happen.” Lila hugs me tightly until Ethan comes back in.

She stands up, and the two of them exchange a hushed conversation in the doorway. After they’re done with their discussion, Ethan rushes upstairs while Lila ducks into the living room to make a phone call.

When she returns to the kitchen, she sits down in the chair beside me.

“Ethan’s going to get everyone off to school before the police show up,” she tells me. “Detective Rannali is going to come here and collect the note, search the area, and dust for prints. He wants you to be here to ask you some questions, though.”

I nod, balling my hands into fists underneath the table, wishing I could go back to Saturday night and have Lyric hold me again.

"I wish the detective was still watching the house. It's like they were waiting for them to leave to make their next more." When I say it aloud, I realize how true that might be.

"You should text Lyric and tell her she'll need to find a ride," Lila says, watching me like a hawk, as if she expects me to crack apart like I used to. "Ayden, everything's going to be okay. We're going to take care of this."

I want to break apart, shatter into pieces, but I'm stronger than that. I can feel the strength where the fresh ink stains my flesh and in the lingering memories of Lyric's lips against mine and the feel of our flesh touching.

Strong.

Strong.

Strong.

I dig my phone out of my pocket and send Lyric a text.

Me: I can't take u to school this morning. Something came up. Sorry.

Lyric: Everything okay?

Me: I'll talk to u at school, okay?

Lyric: Okay.

I know she's probably worried now, but I don't want to give the details of what happened via text.

I put the phone away then spend an hour waiting for the police to show up and another hour after that for them to dust for prints. The entire time, I'm trying to figure out what to do about the note. As risky as it is, I think I need to do what they requested and meet them. Am I terrified out of my goddamn mind? Yes. Will I hate myself if I don't do it? Yes. The biggest problem is going to be convincing Lila to let me go.

After the police are finished dusting for prints and the letter is bagged, Detective Rannali sits down in the living room with Lila and me to ask me some questions—if I've seen anything suspicious, if I know why they sent me the letter.

When he's finished, I have a few questions for him about Sadie and the case. Call it a last resort to the inevitable—that I'm going to have to meet those people at the dock.

"What about those pictures on the website?" I ask. "Have you looked into those? It seems like someone could find them if they went looking for them."

"We've done some research into that, but all the places

have yet to be tracked down." He clicks his pen and presses it to a notepad he fishes from his suit jacket pocket. "And, Ayden, let me stress that you searching for those places is not an option. We believe that was what your brother was doing right before he was murdered. We've had some witnesses give us statements that he was on some sort of mission to find his sister."

"How did he even know she was taken?" I wonder, taken aback.

He went looking for her? Risked everything to find her?

"I think the two of them somehow managed to remain in contact. We pulled your brother's phone records, and Sadie sent him a text a few days before she was taken."

Sadie and her bad feelings. She was always having them and was usually right. She had a bad feeling the day we were taken, warning us that something bad was about to happen.

Sadie.

Sadie.

Sadie.

I'm going to help.

Please, just hold on.

"We're still investigating into it more." He writes something down then glances at Lila. "I have to ask about the amnesia therapy. How has it been coming along? The last update we received was quite a while ago."

"That's because he stopped the therapy," Lila replies curtly, folding her arms. "We didn't see the need for him to keep doing it when there wasn't any progress."

"As of now, that therapy might be the only thing that will help us identify the perpetrators." He seems irked. "I wish you would have informed us that he'd stopped it."

"What about what the note said?" I intervene. "Are we going to talk about that?"

His irritation lessens, as if he were waiting for me to bring it up. "I was planning on mentioning it, yes. I want to know how you feel about it."

"He's not going to meet those people anywhere," Lila snaps. "I'm not going to let him."

"I'm eighteen," I mutter, knowing I'm going to upset her and loathing myself for having to do it.

In the end, this is about saving Sadie.

Lila narrows her eyes at me. "I don't give a shit how old you are. You're my son, and you'll do what you're told."

"Living a life where I could be kidnapped is just as risky," I point out. "I need to do this. Maybe, if I do, it'll lead us to Sadie."

Lila tears up. "I can't let you risk your safety like that. If you go there . . . alone . . ." She shakes her head. "No, I won't let you do it. I can't lose you."

"He wouldn't be alone," the detective chimes in. "We would have officers around the area. The Golden Center Docks couldn't be a more perfect area for this. There are trees and plenty of other places to hide. Plus, it's secluded from the city."

Lila glares at him. "I'm not letting you use him as bait."

"I'm not being used as bait," I insist. "I need to go there for my own sake. Do you know how bad it would eat away at me . . . ? How bad it does eat away at me that I can't save her? She's there, and I'm here. She's suffering, and I'm not."

"Ayden, I . . ." She has no clue what to say to the truth of my words.

"Besides, if we do this, it could lead to some arrests

and maybe put an end to this," I press. "I—we—could all finally have a fucking normal life."

It might be the biggest and longest speech I've ever made, and there's definitely a shock factor to it.

Lila sniffs back tears. "I just want you to live the life you deserve without all this pain."

"Then let me do this for myself. For my sister." I shut my eyes and take a deep breath. "For my brother."

When the room grows quiet, I open my eyes.

She's staring out the window, her eyelashes fluttering against the tears. Detective Rannali catches my gaze and gives me an encouraging look. I don't give a shit about him, though. I'm not doing it for him. I'm doing it for my sister and myself. And for my brother.

"I want assurance that no harm will come to him." She looks over at the detective. "I won't agree to this unless you can give me that."

He nods. "Of course." He tucks the pen and notepad into his pocket. "We're not going to put your son at risk. We'll do this safely, and if anything looks suspicious, then we'll pull him out."

Lila's gaze lands on me. "You have to promise me the same thing. If at any time something seems wrong, you'll leave."

I nod, some of the tension alleviating in my chest, but it's replaced by fear.

Am I really going to do this? See them again? The people who stole my life from me?

Her gaze elevates to the ceiling as she dabs her eyes. "I hope I don't regret this," she mutters. "I don't know what I'd do if I lost you."

Even though I'm not the touchy feely type, it seems like the kind of moment where I should give her a hug, so I wrap an arm around her and give her a pat on the back.

"Thank you . . . and not just for this. For taking me in and making sure that I didn't . . . well, you know."

I'm not sure if she knows just how much I appreciate what they've done for me. Maybe, if my brother and sister could have found this, things would have turned out differently for them. Maybe, if tonight goes well, my sister can still have this in time.

"Oh, Ayden." She pulls me against her, crushing my chest.

Usually, I squirm, but I decide to let her have a moment. Truthfully, I kind of need one, too. Even though I'm strong, I'm still terrified out of my goddamn mind that something will go wrong. Unlike a couple of years ago, I have a lot to lose.

My family.

My music.

A career in music, even.

Most importantly, Lyric. I don't even know if I could function without her, not with how close we've gotten.

She holds me up when I'm falling,

Stills me when I'm tumbling,

Calms me when I'm cracking,

Gives me air when I'm suffocating.

Lyric, she somehow takes the pain away

When everything is crushing down on me.

How I ever lived without her, I have no idea.

The problem is, I'm worried how she's going to react when I tell her what I'm going to do. She flipped out when I told her about the photos. Maybe I should keep this to myself for now.

After the detective leaves to go get his team prepped for tonight, I stay home with Lila and help her clean the house. Scrubbing down the counters and the floors distracts us from the massive cloud hovering above us.

Finally, after the kitchen and living room are sparkling, we sit down at the table to eat some sandwiches.

"I don't want to tell Lyric what I'm doing tonight," I tell her, picking the crust off the bread. "She'll worry about me, and I don't . . ." I swallow hard. "I don't want her to have to go through that."

Lila nods, picking at her food. "I think we should probably keep it from Fiona, Kale, and Everson, too . . ." She shuts her mouth and stares down at the plate. "Ayden, are you sure you want to do this? The police, they'll keep looking for her. They're not going to give up."

"I know they're not going to, but how am I supposed to live with myself if I don't go?"

"This might not go as you plan. You know that, right?"

I nod, sucking in a deep breath. "I know that, but it's worth the risk."

She nods, still staring at her food.

A silence sets in like an ominous doom.

Chapter 16

Ayden

I leave the house before Lyric gets home and drive around town with Lila while she runs some errands. I know, if I see Lyric, then there's a chance I'll break down and tell her everything, so it's a good thing we take off before that can happen. Still, when she sends me a text, I feel like the world's biggest asshole for lying to her.

Lyric: All right, dude, why weren't you at school? What's going on?

Me: Nothing. I didn't feel well, so I stayed home.

Lyric: Why aren't you home now?

Me: Lila took me to the doctor.

Lyric: Is everything all right? Now u have me worried.

Me: Everything's fine. I just have a cold.

There's a pause before the next message buzzes

through.

Lyric: R u sure that's all that's going on? U seem like you're being a little vague and sketchy.

Me: I swear everything's fine. If I'm feeling better by the time I get home, u can come over.

Lyric: Okay.

Her one word response means she's more than likely buying my bullshit. I just hope she isn't too angry when I do go home and have to explain everything to her.

After we finish running errands, Lila drives me to an old diner located near the Golden Center Bridge to meet with Detective Rannali so he can give me a rundown on how the night will go down. He already gave us strict orders to make sure we aren't followed by anyone when we go, and during the thirty-minute drive, Lila is a nervous wreck, constantly checking the rearview mirror, changing lanes, and taking the longest route possible.

By the time we pull up, it's late enough that the sun has set, and the city around us glows against the night. Only an hour left, and then I'll be standing on the dock, facing the people who haunt my nightmares.

Or will I?

Now that I think about it, I can't remember any of their faces nor have I seen any of the people who have been tormenting my life for the last few months. What will happen when I finally see them? Will I know them? Will I remember that I know them? According to some of the stuff the detective has told me, the Soulless Mileas are a decent sized group of people.

"How are you feeling?" Lila asks after she parks the car in front of the diner.

"Fine," I lie, unbuckling my seatbelt. When she presses me with a stern look, I sigh. "Fine. I'm terrified out of my goddamn mind."

"You can always not do it," she says with hope in her eyes. "No one will be upset if you back out."

"That's not true. I'll be upset with myself." I reach for the door handle to let her know I'm going to go through with this.

Sighing, she turns the keys and shuts off the engine. "Just so you know, I'm going to be there, too. I already told Detective Rannali that I'm not going to let you do this unless I can be close."

"All right." I push the door open and climb out of the car.

She gets out, too, and meets me at the front of the car. Then we walk into the diner. The hostess seats us in a booth, tucked away in the corner of the room where the lighting is low. The place has a total of five customers, which is probably why the detective picked this place to meet.

"Anyone hungry?" he asks after the waitress places menus in front of us and leaves.

I shake my head. "Not really."

Lila reaches over and flips open the menu. "You're going to eat. I don't want you doing this on an empty stomach. You need your strength."

Giving her what she wants, I order a plate of fries and a soda. She orders nothing for herself, and the detective asks for a glass of water.

"So, I first want to assure you that the location of the dock couldn't be any better," the detective starts after our drinks have been delivered. "There are trees and bushes surrounding it, and there's also an old, vacant building nearby. My team has already scoped out the place and set everything up. Nothing appeared suspicious, so I have no reason to believe this won't go smoothly."

"The note said to come alone, though," Lila reminds him. "Aren't you worried that's going to cause problems?"

"The only problem I foresee is that no one shows up." He reaches for his water and takes a sip. "There was no threat to the note, though, which I found a little odd. I'm guessing they assume Ayden will just listen to them."

"But I don't even get why they want him to meet them," Lila says, folding her arms on the table. "What exactly is the point of making him come out here to meet them?"

The detective exchanges a look with me from across the table. I can tell he's thinking the same thing.

"I know this isn't what you want to hear"—he leans back in the booth—"but we believe it's their way of coaxing Ayden out to a desolate place so they can try to take him without making a scene." When Lila's eyes widen, he adds, "Don't worry. We're not going to allow that to happen. I have ten of my best men all surrounding the dock."

"You better not mess this up," Lila says, being all hardcore. "If anything happens at all, I'll track you down and cut off your balls."

The detective appears highly amused by the threat. "Duly noted." He turns to me. "I need to go over a few things with you. First and most importantly, under no circumstances are you to get into a vehicle with anyone."

"You think they're going to ask me to do that?" I ask, stirring my soda with my straw.

"It's a possibility, yes."

"Can't you just arrest them when they show up?" Lila absentmindedly steals a fry off my plate and pops it into her mouth.

He puts his hands out in front of him being very down-to-business. "We will arrest them, but we have to be careful and move slowly so we don't spook them. We want to make sure that this ends with us getting Sadie back. You have to understand, these people aren't your typical criminals. They have heavy beliefs that bind them to each other. Cracking down on them and trying to get them to out the rest of the group isn't something that's going to easily happen. In fact, from all the information I've collected on them throughout the case, more than likely, they'd easily go to jail to keep their secrets."

Lila swallows hard. "All right, I'll trust your judgment, then."

"Thank you," he says. "Now, Ayden, I want you to listen carefully."

He gives me rule after rule: no acting spooked, keep calm, no trying to take matters into my own hands. He acts as though I'm going to flip out when the person shows up and try to kill them. While I briefly ponder the idea, I would never do something like that.

By the time he's given me the rundown, there's ten minutes left before go time. I've eaten probably a total of five fries and feel sick to my stomach.

"Are you ready for this?" he asks me after he pays the bill.

I shrug and then nod. "As ready as I'll ever be."

The detective and Lila leave the diner first, getting in his unmarked car and driving down to the location. I climb in Lila's car and remain in the parking lot for five more minutes before backing out. Then it takes me three minutes to get to Golden Center Docks and another two to get out of the car.

I reach the dock that stretches out over the water with no time to spare, which is exactly what I was hoping for. The last thing I want is to be standing out here in the open, terrified to fucking death.

The water laps under the wooden dock I'm standing

on, and the trees enclosing the area sway with the wind. The sky is dark, the moon full, and the stars bright. In the distance, I spot the building the detective mentioned. Every now and then, I hear a noise and wonder if it's the person meeting me here or if it's the police. I can't really tell. In fact, I can't really tell much of anything other than I'm edgy as shit.

Finally, at around a quarter after ten, I spot movement from the path that leads down to the dock. I turn and watch as the figure descends the shallow hill and heads straight for me. My muscles seize up, and I want to run, but force myself to stay put.

When the person reaches the edge of the dock, I realize I'm cornered. The only place for me to go is in the water. Whoever it is has all the control, which instantly makes me think it's someone from the Soulless Mileas.

They slowly make their way toward me, each step premeditated. As they get closer, the moonlight casts across them, and my jaw drops. They're wearing a red raincoat with the hood pulled over their head and black rain boots.

She stops halfway down the dock, leaving at least ten to fifteen feet between us.

"Hello, Ayden."

"You're the person who was at that house," I say with my eyes trained on her. "The one who warned me the place wasn't safe."

"It wasn't safe," she answers calmly in the same gruff voice she used that day. "It wasn't time for you to go yet."

A chill slithers up my spine.

"What do you want?" I ask, daring to take a step toward her. "Why did you ask me to come here?"

"I didn't ask you to come," she replies, taking a step back. "You were chosen to come."

"You were chosen, Ayden," she whispers in my ear. "You were chosen for this since the day you were born."

I blink from the memory and step toward her, my legs shaking. "It was you . . ."

"Close your eyes," she says. "This is going to hurt."

I stop in the middle of the dock. "You were there."

She shakes her head. "No, I wasn't. I'm here now, though."

She speaks like everyone else in my memories, her words wrapped in riddles.

"Tell me why I'm here," I demand, my voice echoing around us.

She glances at the water behind me, and then her gaze slides to the trees. "Ayden, you've been a bad boy." Her eyes land back on me. "You were supposed to come alone."

Shit.

She turns and races off down the path toward the direction she came. I run after her without thinking, refusing to let her get away. Tree branches whip at my face as I keep my eyes on her, tracking her as she swings left then right before veering into the trees.

I dive in after her, the leaves and branches thick around my face. I know somewhere in the midst of the trees there are officers, but I can't hear or see anything other than the woman laughing from somewhere.

"You want to know why we picked you?" she asks, her voice sounding as if it's coming at me in every direction. "You want to know why?"

"No." I whirl left then right, scanning the area for her. "I want to know what you've done with my sister."

"Your sister?" she asks with a cackle. "I don't think I know who you're talking about."

"You're lying," I growl, stumbling deeper into the trees. "Tell me where she is."

"Hmmm . . . Let me think. Locked in a house, swallowed by the darkness, where no one has ever killed, yet blood stains the floors and the walls."

"Fuck you!" I shout, lunging in the direction of where it sounds like her voice is coming from. Instead, I end up bumping into a tree.

I hear the sound of officers yelling my name from somewhere close by and shout out, "I'm over here!"

"And here's another little secret I'll let you in on." Her voice floats from the trees ahead of me. "Your blood is tied to us, Ayden. And not because your mother gave us to you. Your blood has tied you to us from the moment you were conceived." Footsteps dance around me. "Ever wonder who your real father is?"

"No." I cover my ears with my hands as I sink to my knees.

"Ever wonder why we chose you?" she whispers in my ear. "Ever wonder why your mother gave you up so easily?"

"No. No. No." Rage crashes through me as I jump to my feet. "I'm not going to let you get away with this."

"We already have," she whispers from right behind me. Then something hits me hard on the back of the head.

Love, love, love.

I never got a chance to say I love her.

My eyes slip shut as I begin to fall.

Then everything goes black.

Chapter 17

Lyric

Something's wrong. I could tell from the moment Ayden sent me the text this morning. The worry only magnifies when I step foot into my house. For starters, both my parents are home, and Ethan is here along with the three youngest of the Gregorys. When I ask them what's up, they give me a vague, "We're just hanging out" answer.

Ayden also didn't show up for school. He said he was sick, but I'm not buying it. Something's definitely up.

"So, when are you guys going to fess up?" I announce while everyone's sitting around the table, eating pizza.

"Fess up to what?" my dad replies, acting all breezy.

"Whatever's going on with Ayden." I pick a pepperoni off a slice and drop it back into the box.

"Nothing's going on," Ethan says, staring distractedly at his pizza slice.

"You're lying. I can tell." My eyes travel across him, my dad, then land on my mom.

She shakes her head. "Lyric, nothing's wrong. Ayden's just sick and went to the doctor." She checks the time on the microwave. "Lila did say she had to run a few errands, and they were going to be a little late."

"Whatever. Don't tell me, then." I finish off my pizza then chill in the living room for a while with my sketchbook.

I work on a drawing of a tattoo I'm thinking about getting until around nine thirty or so when Fiona and Everson walk in. They have backpacks in their hands and frowns on their faces.

"Something's definitely up," Everson says as he drops his pack on the floor and sinks back in the chair. "It's too late for them to be gone."

I thrum my fingers on the top of my thighs. "Did Ayden seem sick this morning?"

Fiona shakes her head as she unzips her backpack. "No, he seemed fine." She pulls out a thick textbook. "My parents seemed freaked out, though. My dad was acting like a weirdo the entire drive to school, and he gave us this huge lecture about being careful and keeping an eye out for anything weird today."

"It probably has something to do with the fact that the police were at our house this morning." Kale appears in the doorway with a slice of pizza in his hand.

I turn the volume of the stereo down. "How do you know the police were at your house?"

He shrugs, sinking down into a chair. "I was hanging out at one of my friend's houses across the street, and his mom asked me about it."

I bite down on my lip and pull out my phone to send Ayden a text.

Me: When r u going to b home?

When he doesn't answer, an uneasy feeling gnaws in the pit of my stomach. I know he's told me time and time again not to worry about him, but I can't help it. I love him, and not knowing where he is drives me crazy.

I get lost in my thoughts as I flip through songs while everyone works on their homework. I've always had a rather overactive imagination, and it conjures up a thousand different horrible scenarios of what could be going on.

When my mother walks into the room and motions me to come over, I suddenly realize that maybe my imagination was right. Perhaps something terrible has happened.

She points at Fiona, Kale, and Everson, then puts her fingers to her lips, indicating for me to be quiet before leaving the room. I causally get up and wind around the sofa.

"Where are you going?" Fiona asks, glancing up from the textbook.

"To get a snack," I reply, hoping I sound calm.

"Grab me something, too, would ya?"

I nod. "Sure."

She smiles and returns to her homework while I hurry and sneak out of the room. When I get into the kitchen, my mother is sitting at the table with her phone clutched in her hand, and my dad and Uncle Ethan are hurrying for the back door.

"What's wrong?" I ask.

My dad motions for me to come with them. "We need to go to the hospital."

I feel as though someone has punched me in the stomach and knocked the wind out of me. "What happened?"

Worry is written all over his face as he grabs the car keys off the counter. "There's been an accident. I'll explain on the way. We need to go."

Bile burns at the back of my throat as I slip on my shoes and follow them out the door. We climb into my dad's 1969 Chevelle, and he breaks almost every traffic law as he flies down the street and onto the freeway.

"Would someone please tell me what's going on?" I finally say after ten very long minutes go by.

My dad glances at Ethan who looks as though he's about to be sick.

"Go ahead and tell her." He grabs his phone out of his pocket and sends a text. "She's going to find out eventually."

Sighing, my dad focuses on the road and begins telling me a horrible story about a letter and a meeting and basically a plan that consisted of Ayden risking his life.

By the time he's finished, I almost ask him to pull over so I can throw up.

"But he's all right?" I ask Ethan, sliding forward in the seat to look at him.

"I'm not sure. Lila . . . her text said . . ." He shakes his head. "I never should have let him do it."

"Knowing Ayden, he would have done it without you," I tell him. "I think he believes it's his job to save his sister."

"I know." Ethan's phone vibrates in his hand, and he

glances down at the screen. When he sighs in relief, I know it has to be good news. "I just got an update from Lila. Ayden's okay. He hurt his head and had to get stitches, but other than that, he's going to be fine."

I breathe freely for the first time as I lean back in the seat. I hadn't realized how worried I was until now. Worried more than I ever have been.

Love, it's like a drug
I can't live without.
I thought I was stronger.
But love, it owns me now.
Without him, I feel so lost.
Without him, I don't feel whole.
Love, love, love,
What have you done to me?

Chapter 18

Ayden

Despite Lila's many protests, after I get the stitches put in my head, I talked to Detective Rannali who has been waiting in the emergency room with us. She watches him like a hawk from the corner of the room, ready to yell at him the moment he says something that pisses her off even more.

"Are you sure you didn't get a positive ID on the woman?" He pulls the curtain shut to give us some privacy.

I shake my head. "All I know is that she was wearing a red raincoat and black rain boots. She had a voice like a heavy smoker." I reach up to scratch my head then remember I can't because of the stitches. "I know she was the woman who was at the house, though. The one who warned me about being there."

"Can you recount what was said by her?" he asks,

grabbing his pen and notebook from his pocket.

I replay everything I can remember her saying, and he writes it all down.

"I don't get how you guys didn't catch her, though," I say after I'm finished. "She was right there with me in the trees."

"We still have a team out searching the area," he says. "But I have a theory that she might have had a boat nearby. We have some people out on the water, searching, and we did find a red raincoat tossed in the bushes near the shore-line."

"You said he was going to be safe," Lila interrupts, crossing her arms and staring him down. "And that nothing bad was going to happen, yet the woman got away, and my son's in the hospital."

"And I'm greatly sorry about that." He clicks his pen and tucks it away. "But I also told you that I couldn't pre-dict everything that was going to happen, only what I hoped would happen."

She shakes her head, enraged. "You lied."

"Why do you think she said that thing about my real father?" I slide off the bed and plant my feet on the ground, steadying myself as the world starts to spin underneath me.

"Take it easy, Ayden." Lila holds onto my arm. "The doctor said you need to move slowly for a little while."

"I'm not sure," the detective answers, stuffing his notepad back into his pocket. "Do you know who your real father is?"

"I thought I did." I lean against the bed for support. "But my mom was the kind of woman who might have lied about stuff like that."

He mulls over something, and I know what he's thinking, because it's probably the same thing I am. That my real father might have something to do with this. He might be part of the Soulless Mileas.

"I'm going to do a little searching into you," he says, drawing the curtain back. "I'll keep you updated, but in the meantime, I'm going to send a detective to keep an eye on Ayden."

His words don't soften Lila at all. In fact, her face reddens with anger.

"If this escalates into something worse . . ." She jabs a finger at him.

"I know. I know. You'll cut off my balls." He swings around her and heads for the doors that lead to the waiting room.

After he's gone, Lila turns to me. "'How are you feeling?" She squints at my face to examine my eyes. "The doctor says we need to keep an eye out for a concussion."

"I know. I was right here, remember?" I ask, starting for the door.

"I know. That was a test to see how your memory is." She walks ahead of me and pushes the door open so I can go through.

"My memory's fine." But that's not the truth.

I may be able to remember tonight, but I still can't remember that time in the house. Part of me wonders now if the reason why I blocked it all out isn't just because of the trauma and horrible things that happened to me in that house. Maybe my mind is trying to protect me from the pain of who was behind it all.

Could it be my real father who chose to break me, his own flesh and blood?

As soon as I step foot into the waiting room, my worries momentarily vanish, and all my thoughts center on one thing or person, anyway.

"Ayden." Lyric's eyes light up when she sees me. She

sprints across the room, pushing people out of her way to get to me. When she reaches me, she throws her arms around me and almost knocks me to the ground. "I was so worried . . . I don't even . . ." She stops talking and holds me tightly.

"Careful, Lyric," Lila says from beside us. "He might have a concussion."

Lyric starts to pull back, but I place my hand on the small of her back and press her closer. "She's fine," I tell Lila.

I won't let her go.

Not until she knows.

Ethan gives me a pat on the back while Lyric remains latched on to me.

"I'm glad you're okay." Her eyes are red like she's been crying.

I've been crying, too, but not because I've been worried for my safety. I cried during the ride to the hospital because the woman got away. My hope to find Sadie got away.

Lyric and I remain joined at the hip as we pile into her dad's car. Lila rides with us, too, because she refuses to let me out of her sight.

"I'll come back for the car in the morning," she says as she climbs into the backseat with Lyric and me.

Ethan nods in agreement as Mr. Scott drives forward and out onto the road. Everyone stays pretty quiet during the drive, and the sound of the tires and the lull of the radio fills up the silence.

Lyric keeps her arms around me and her head resting above my heart. I count to ten under my breath, over and over again. Not because she's touching me. Not because I'm having a panic attack. But because the need to tell her how I feel is about to combust inside me.

I thought I was going to die tonight,

Be buried in the trees

Beneath the stars and the moon

For only the sky to see.

My body would sink into the dirt

And be stilled in the silence forever.

And in the midst of my mind,

I knew I'd never be able to tell her.

It's well past midnight by the time we make it home. Everson, Kale, and Fiona are asleep on the Scott's couch and floor, and Lyric's mom looks worried out of her mind.

"Let them sleep," Mrs. Scott says to Lila. "I'll call you when they wake up tomorrow."

Lila nods gratefully. She has bags under her eyes, her blonde hair has slipped from her braid, and she looks drained dry. Even Ethan doesn't look in that great of shape.

I want to make this easy on them so they can get some rest, but there's something I have to do first.

"Can I talk to Lyric for a moment?" I ask as Lila leans down to kiss Fiona on the head.

"Of course." She moves to Kale, pulling the blanket over him. "Just make it quick, please."

I nod then steer Lyric toward the stairway.

"Where are we going?" she asks as I take her hand and lead her up the stairs.

"I have to tell you something." I move slowly; otherwise, my head throbs. My heart, on the other hand, races violently inside my chest as I mentally go over what I'm going to say to her. Preparing doesn't do any good, though, because the moment we make it into her room, and she looks at me with her stunning green eyes, my mind blanks out on me.

"I-I love you?" I stutter, sounding more like I'm asking a question than declaring my feelings for her. As soon as the words leave my lips, I want to smack myself in the head. "God, that sounded awful."

"No, it didn't. It was perfect." Her hands glide up my chest, and she links her arms around my neck. "I love you, too."

I seal my lips to hers, kissing her deliberately, savoring the taste, feel, scent, the warmth of her as I back her to the bed and lay her down. I know we don't have a lot of time, but I need a moment to feel her beneath me, know she's here.

Know that I'm still here.

I thought I was never going to have this again. Now that I know what it feels like to think I've lost it—her—I don't know what I was so afraid of. Being with her is better than music, poetry, words spilled on pages.

This is . . .

Perfect.

"I need you to do me a favor," I say, pushing back to look down at her.

She nods, her lips swollen from the kiss, her chest heaving as she struggles to catch her breath. "Whatever you need, I'm here for you."

She says exactly what I knew she would say. I just hope she'll keep her word.

"I'm going to call Dr. Gardingdale and make an appointment to do the experimental therapy, and I need you to be there for me, because I know Lila's not going to. Not after tonight."

"Ay"—she hesitates—"are you sure that's a good idea after what just happened?"

"That's the thing." I push up, sit down on her bed, and pull my knee up to rest my arm on my leg. "Tonight could have been avoided if I had just done the damn therapy to begin with."

Lyric sits up beside me, combing her hair into place. "You know I'll be there for you if you need me." She lays her hand over mine and threads our fingers together. "I just need you to be sure you want to do this."

I turn and look her directly in the eyes so she'll know how truthful I'm being. "I want to do this."

She grasps onto my hand and shuts her eyes. "Then I'll be there for you."

"Thank you." I lean in and kiss her before moving off the bed and retrieving my phone from my pocket.

"You're calling him now?" she asks, standing to her

feet.

I nod as I dial his office number. "I'll leave a message on his phone, but I need to do it now; otherwise, it'll drive me crazy."

I put the phone up to my ear, taking deep breaths and preparing myself for what I'm about to do. The cards have shifted now that I know my real father might be involved, and I'm even more terrified of what's locked away in the box in my mind.

I have to do it now more than ever.

I know what the risks are. Shock. More memory loss. Heart complications. There's a short list of other side effects, as well.

But it's time to take that risk. It's time for me to face my demons head on and find out what really happened to my siblings and me in that house. And who did it to us.

About the Author

Jessica Sorensen is a *New York Times* and *USA Today* bestselling author that lives in the snowy mountains of Wyoming. When she's not writing, she spends her time reading and hanging out with her family.

Other books by Jessica Sorensen:

The Coincidence Series:

The Coincidence of Callie and Kayden

The Redemption of Callie and Kayden

The Destiny of Violet and Luke

The Probability of Violet and Luke

The Certainty of Violet and Luke

The Resolution of Callie and Kayden

Seth & Grayson (Coming Soon)

The Secret Series:

The Prelude of Ella and Micha

The Secret of Ella and Micha

The Forever of Ella and Micha

The Temptation of Lila and Ethan

The Ever After of Ella and Micha

Lila and Ethan: Forever and Always

Ella and Micha: Infinitely and Always

The Shattered Promises Series:

Shattered Promises

Fractured Souls

Unbroken

Broken Visions

Scattered Ashes (Coming Soon)

Breaking Nova Series:

Breaking Nova

Saving Quinton

Delilah: The Making of Red

Nova and Quinton: No Regrets

Tristan: Finding Hope

Wreck Me

Ruin Me

The Fallen Star Series (YA):

The Fallen Star

The Underworld

The Vision

The Promise

The Fallen Souls Series (spin off from The Fallen Star):

The Lost Soul

The Evanescence

The Darkness Falls Series:

Darkness Falls

Darkness Breaks

Darkness Fades

The Death Collectors Series (NA and YA):

Ember X and Ember

Cinder X and Cinder

Spark X and Cinder (Coming Soon)

The Sins Series:

Seduction & Temptation

Sins & Secrets

Unbeautiful Series:

Unbeautiful

Untamed

Unraveling Series:

Unraveling You

Raveling You

Awakening You

Standalones

The Forgotten Girl

Coming Soon:

Entranced

Steel & Bones

Connect with me online:

jessicasorensen.com

http://www.facebook.com/pages/Jessica-Sorensen/165335743524509

https://twitter.com/#!/jessFallenStar

CPSIA information can be obtained at www.ICGtesting.com
Printed in the USA
LVOW07s1115170915

454575LV00003B/85/P